20p

D0493925

Nancy Drew
in
The Clue in the Crossword Cipher

This Armada book belongs to:

The Nancy Drew Mystery Stories

The Clue in the Crossword Cipher

Carolyn Keene

Armada

First published in the U.K. in 1971 by
William Collins Sons & Co. Ltd., London and Glasgow.
This edition was first published in Armada in 1973 by
Fontana Paperbacks,
14 St. James's Place, London SW1A 1PS.

This impression 1982.

© MCMLXVII Grosset & Dunlap, Inc. All rights reserved
under International and Pan-American copyright conventions.
Published pursuant to agreement with Grosset & Dunlap, Inc.,
New York, N.Y., U.S.A.

© 1971 in Great Britain and the British Commonwealth (except
Canada) by William Collins Sons & Co. Ltd.

Printed in Great Britain by
Love & Malcomson Ltd., Brighton Road,
Redhill, Surrey.

The author gratefully acknowledges the assistance of Mr.
Roberto Kennedy of Lima, Peru, in supplying the Quechuan
words and phrases used in this story.

CONDITIONS OF SALE:
This book is sold subject to the condition that
it shall not, by way of trade or otherwise, be lent,
re-sold, hired out or otherwise circulated without
the publisher's prior consent in any form of
binding or cover other than that in which it is
published and without a similar condition
including this condition being imposed on the
subsequent purchaser.

CONTENTS

·1·

The Monkey Mystery

"This is what I want you to solve, Nancy. I call it my monkey mystery."

The speaker was beautiful Carla Ponte from Lima, Peru. She had large dark-brown eyes, shoulder-length black hair and olive skin. Her visitor was attractive Nancy Drew, fair-skinned, blue-eyed and titian-haired. Both girls were eighteen.

Carla pointed to a round wooden plaque about fifteen inches in diameter which hung on the wall of her bedroom. The wood was very old, but the carving on it fairly clear.

"It's an outline of a monkey with part of his tail cut off," said Nancy, "and several lines spread from one side of him to the edge of the plaque. You think this design may be a clue to some great secret? Perhaps a treasure?"

"Yes. The plaque has been in my family for three hundred years," Carla replied in her delightful Spanish-accented English. "But it disappeared. Then, about twenty years ago my father found it in my great-grandfather's trunk. But nobody has ever been able to work out the significance of the carving."

As Nancy gazed at the walking monkey with its arched back, Carla took the plaque from the wall and laid it reverse side up on a table.

"This side is even more intriguing," she said.

Down the centre was a series of gouged-out spaces with two similar crossing sets. Radiating from the middle was a spiralling group of lines which extended to the very outside of the plaque.

"This is fascinating!" Nancy remarked. "Oh, Carla, I'd love to work on your mystery. But I'm a little embarrassed even to try when others have worked on it for so many years."

Carla gave Nancy an affectionate squeeze. "From what I have heard of cases you have solved, I am sure you will work out this one. What bothers me is that if the plaque is a clue to a treasure buried long ago, by this time someone may have found it."

"We'll have to take that chance," said Nancy. "The first thing I'd like to do is examine this under my magnifying glass. How about coming home with me to dinner and bringing along the plaque?"

"That sounds wonderful!" said Carla. "I will tell my aunt."

While in River Heights, Carla was living with an aunt and uncle. She had just graduated from secretarial college and would return to Lima in a few days.

The two girls went downstairs to speak to Mrs Renshaw, a friend of the Drews.

"I'm happy to have Carla go with you," she said, "but I don't want her to come home alone. She had a bad scare one night. Mr Renshaw and I will drive over to get her."

"Oh, that won't be necessary," Nancy said quickly. "My father and I will bring her back."

Mrs Renshaw looked relieved. "Probably I should

explain why I'm concerned. Carla recently has been followed several times."

"You mean by a man?" Nancy asked.

Mrs Renshaw nodded. "There is more to the story than that."

"Oh please, Auntie," Carla protested. "I am sure you worry unnecessarily."

Her aunt continued with the story. "Only yesterday Carla received a very strange message in the mail. It was a sheet of paper on to which letters cut from newspaper headlines had been pasted. The message was, '*Cuidado con el gato*'. "

Carla explained, "It means, 'Beware of the cat'. "

"How strange!" said Nancy.

"We cannot figure it out," Carla said. "My aunt and uncle have no cat and there is not a bothersome one in the neighbourhood."

Nancy looked off into space. Having solved many mysteries, her thoughts immediately flew to the idea that *el gato* was a person.

To herself she said, "He may be the man who has been following Carla and someone is trying to warn her against him." Aloud she said, "Carla, could El Gato refer to something at your home in Lima?"

Carla said that the Pontes had no cat and she was at a loss to explain what the warning meant. "I am not going to worry about it, though, because I shall be leaving for home soon."

"Good idea," said Nancy.

She suggested that the girls start for the Drews'. They said goodbye to Carla's aunt and went outside. The Renshaw house stood on a slope overlooking the Muskoka River. The girls gazed towards the water as they walked to Nancy's convertible. Carla was clutching the plaque tightly.

In the driveway she skidded on some loose gravel, and while trying to regain her balance, let go of the plaque. It flew through the air, landed on the edge of the slope, then began rolling down rapidly.

Carla gave a cry of dismay. "Oh, I mustn't lose it!"

Instantly Nancy took off after the fast-disappearing object. Though the way down was precarious, she had almost caught up with the plaque when it bounced off a stone. The momentum sent the ancient piece of wood sailing through the air and into the water, some twelve feet below.

"My precious heirloom!" Carla cried out. "It will be lost!"

Within seconds Nancy had kicked off her pumps and made a shallow dive into the river. She surfaced not far from the plaque, which already was being swept along by the swift current. With strong strokes she overtook it. Grasping the plaque firmly, she made for shore.

When Nancy reached the river bank, Carla exclaimed, "Oh, how can I ever thank you! I am terribly sorry I dropped the plaque. We will go back to the house and you can put on some dry clothes."

"I'll be all right," Nancy insisted. "It isn't far to my home. I'll keep the windows of my car closed so I won't catch cold."

Fifteen minutes later she was pulling into the Drews' circular driveway. The front door was opened by Mrs Hannah Gruen, the pleasant, middle-aged housekeeper, who had helped to rear Nancy since the death of Mrs Drew. She was delighted to hear that Carla would stay to dinner.

Within seconds Nancy had dived to rescue the heirloom

"We have something interesting to show you," said Nancy as she led the way to the dining room and laid the plaque on the table. Carla explained its origin to the housekeeper, while Nancy ran upstairs to change her clothes and get the magnifying glass which had served her so well in solving other mysteries. As soon as she returned, the young sleuth gazed through the glass at the monkey side of the plaque.

"I see something down here in the corner," she announced. "It's a word—perhaps a name. It spells A-G-U-I-L-A-R."

"Oh!" Carla cried out. "That was the name of an ancestor of ours. He was a great artist. I never knew his name was on here."

"Then he must have carved these figures," said Nancy. "What became of him?"

"He disappeared from Lima," Carla answered. "No one ever heard of him again."

Nancy could not detect anything further which she had not seen before. Now she turned the plaque over.

"Umm!" she murmured. "I see something here."

"What is it?" Carla asked eagerly.

"The centre carvings are parts of words," Nancy deduced. "I can barely make out some of the letters reading from the top down. They seem to be part of a crossword puzzle. Here, Carla, see what you can make out of it."

The girl from Lima took the glass and gazed through it. Excitedly she exclaimed, "The first four letters down are *mono!* That is Spanish for monkey. I cannot make out anything else. The markings are too indistinct."

Though Nancy felt she had made a start on solving

the mystery, she realized there was a long way to go before discovering its real significance.

Hannah asked Nancy to set the table. Dinner was to be early because the housekeeper had made arrangements to go to the cinema with a friend.

A few minutes later Mr Drew came in. He was a trim, handsome man and a successful lawyer. After greeting Carla and hearing about the mystery, he smiled. "I knew it wouldn't be long before Nancy would become involved with some enigma. This one sounds like a real challenge."

"I believe the clue to it," said Nancy, "is in the crossword cipher."

Later, when it was time for Carla to go home, she suggested that Nancy keep the plaque and work on it.

Nancy's eyes twinkled. "You have a lot of faith in me," she said. "I'll help you all I can before you go back to Lima. But please don't be too disappointed if I don't succeed."

Suddenly Carla's beautiful big brown eyes lighted up. "Nancy, I have an idea. Will you and your friends, Bess and George, come to South America with me? Then you would have more time to work on the mystery."

"I'm sure I'll need it. This is a marvellous invitation. Thank you. When do you leave?"

"Day after tomorrow."

Nancy looked inquiringly at her father, but before he could speak, Carla went on, "Even if there were no mystery to solve, I would love to have you all visit me. Peru is a fascinating place. We have ancient Indian ruins, Spanish palaces, exotic things to buy and eat. Do come!"

"It certainly sounds exciting," said Nancy. "I'd love to accept. What do you say, Dad?"

Mr Drew looked at his daughter with amusement in his eyes. "How could I refuse? And I hope Bess and George can go along." Nancy promised to call the girls early the next morning.

Presently she and her father left the house with Carla. They took the Peruvian girl back to the Renshaws, and after talking with them a few minutes, the Drews drove home.

"I'm going to work on that plaque a little more before I go to bed," said Nancy. "But first, can I get you something to eat or drink, Dad?"

"No thanks," he said. "I'd like to take a look at those strange markings myself."

They walked into the dining room and turned on the light. Both stopped short. They had left the plaque on the table. Now it was gone!

·2·

A Bit of Judo

"CARLA's precious plaque!" Nancy exclaimed. "It must have been stolen!"

As she berated herself for leaving the object in plain sight, Mr Drew said, "Maybe Hannah put it away."

"No, Dad. Hannah left the house first and I know the plaque was right here on the table when you and I went out."

The lawyer patted his daughter on the shoulder. "This is more of a mystery than I thought it was going to be. I suppose it will delay your trip to Lima."

"Oh, how can I tell Carla?" Nancy said, a catch in her voice. "But I'll have to do it."

As she started for the telephone, her father said, "Perhaps we should call the police first. But before we do that, let's look round and see if anything else has been stolen."

He and Nancy examined the drawer of silverware. Nothing was missing. They searched the rooms downstairs and those on the first floor. Nothing seemed to have been stolen.

Nancy and her father were about to telephone the police when they heard a key in the front door lock and for a moment the two stiffened. They were relieved when Hannah Gruen walked in.

18

"Hello," she said cheerfully. "The film was excellent. You must see it." As she noted the glum faces of her employer and his daughter, she asked, "Is something the matter?"

"Oh, Hannah, the plaque has been stolen from the dining-room table!" Nancy told her.

The housekeeper, instead of looking shocked, remained calm. "I'm sorry I upset you," she said. "During intermission I got to worrying that you might not have put the plaque away. Since Carla was followed and received that strange note about a cat, I hurried home and hid the plaque."

She went directly to the bottom drawer of the dining-room buffet and pulled the object from beneath a pile of table mats.

Mr Drew sat down in a chair and burst into laughter. "Hannah, you're wiser and more sensible than either of us. Here am I a lawyer and Nancy has quite a reputation as an amateur detective, and you're the only one who thought of hiding this valuable old object."

His laughter was so contagious that Nancy and Hannah joined in. Finally the housekeeper said, "I think this calls for a little celebration—a midnight snack. How about chocolate frosted apple-sauce cake and glasses of milk?"

"Sounds good," said Nancy. "I'll help you."

The family lingered for half an hour, watching the late news on TV, then went to bed. Nancy slept soundly but was up early, determined to work on the crossword cipher. Using a Spanish dictionary, she tried to work out what the missing letters might be, but finally gave up.

Nancy had just gone into the kitchen to start breakfast when Hannah Gruen came downstairs. By the time everything was ready, Mr Drew appeared. Nancy told him of her fruitless attempt to solve the cipher.

He said with a smile, "But you won't stop work on it yet!"

"No indeed," Nancy replied.

After the lawyer had left for his office, she went to the phone to tell Bess Marvin and George Fayne of Carla's invitation. Both girls were thrilled and said they would come as soon as possible to get more details.

George added, "I may be a little late. You know this is my morning for a judo lesson."

Nancy laughed. "Be sure to learn something that will be useful in our detective work!"

George chuckled. "You mean like tossing a villain off a cliff?"

Two hours later Bess and George, who were cousins, arrived. Bess, a blonde with attractive dimples, was slightly overweight and always being teased about it. Her slogan was, "I'll start dieting tomorrow."

George was the antithesis of her cousin. She was an attractive brunette with a slender figure, and was interested in many sports.

The two cousins were intrigued by the ancient plaque. Bess giggled. "I love that monkey on it—he's so nice and awkward."

"I'm more interested in the other side," said George. "I wish all those letters weren't missing."

Nancy was about to hand her the magnifying glass when the front doorbell rang. She went to answer it. A man about thirty years old stood on the porch.

"Are you Miss Drew?"

"Yes." At once the stranger turned back one side of his coat. Pinned to the lining was a badge, saying, "Detective, River Heights Police Department."

"May I come in?" he asked.

As Nancy admitted him, he said, "My name is Harry Wallace. I have a court order for the plaque which you have." From a pocket he produced a piece of paper to confirm his statement, but did not hand it to her to read.

Bess and George, overhearing the conversation, walked into the hall. Bess was carrying the plaque.

"But I don't understand," said Nancy. "Why would the police want this private property?"

Harry Wallace shrugged. "How should I know? When I get an order I just carry it out. Give me the plaque and I'll be going."

Nancy's suspicions were aroused. She did not like the man's looks nor the abrupt manner in which he was demanding the plaque.

Looking him straight in the eye, she said, "I'm not giving this to you without further proof. Please sit down while I telephone Chief McGinnis."

Wallace's eyes flashed. "Young lady," he said angrily, "you're entirely too fresh for your own good. You give me that plaque and no back talk!"

The next instant he grabbed it from Bess's arms and made a dash for the front door. He did not get far. George, quick as a flash, stepped forward and with a neat flip tossed him over her shoulder. He landed on his back on the carpet and lay there in utter astonishment.

Bess began to giggle and picked up the plaque which had fallen to the floor. But Nancy was worried. She might be in trouble over what had happened. Suppose the man really was a police detective!

She helped Wallace up and escorted him to the front door. He went out meekly, saying nothing more about taking the plaque with him.

After the door was closed, George remarked, "Well, there wasn't any cliff, but I hope you liked the way I tossed that villain out of our lives."

Bess looked scared. "He may take revenge instead."

Nancy said, "Wallace might even be the man who has been following Carla recently."

"And sent that warning note about 'the cat'?" Bess queried.

"Could be."

Nancy immediately telephoned her friend Police Chief McGinnis. After telling him what had happened, Bess and George saw Nancy nodding her head in agreement as she listened. Finally she said, "He's about thirty, dark-complexioned, has close-cut black hair, and is extremely thin."

Presently the young sleuth said goodbye and put down the phone. Turning to her friends, Nancy said, "Harry Wallace is a phoney. He's not on the detective squad. Chief McGinnis is going to put out an alarm for him at once. By the way, George," she said with a grin, "the chief thanks you for using a little judo on that impostor."

"Hypers!" George cried, rubbing her hands together gleefully. "The first villain in this mystery. I wonder how many more we'll encounter."

Bess quickly spoke up. "I hope he's the only one. I want to help solve the crossword cipher mystery, but I can get along without people like him!"

Later that day Bess and George telephoned Nancy to tell her they had received permission from their parents to go to Lima. Carla was overjoyed when she heard the good news.

"We will have a marvellous time," she promised.

Fortunately, Nancy and the cousins had passports. Mr Drew made the arrangements for the flight. The girls would leave early the following morning from River Heights and fly to New York City. From there they would take a jet to South America.

"With Harry Wallace at large," he said, "I think it would be best if you girls leave River Heights unobtrusively."

"How can we do that?" Nancy asked.

"By staying at the airport motel tonight. Bess's and George's families can drive them separately and should be sure they're not being followed. Carla's uncle can take her to the motel and you—" Mr Drew grinned. "I believe Ned Nickerson is coming here this evening?"

Nancy blushed. Ned was a special friend who attended Emerson College.

"Yes, Ned is coming to have dinner with us. He'll be glad to take me to the airport."

The tall, good-looking football player arrived at six o'clock. After warm greetings he said to Nancy, "So you're taking off again to solve another mystery. Can't you fix things so that I could go along?"

Nancy smiled. "I wish I could. Now I have to depend on George and her judo to take care of trouble-makers."

She had already packed for the trip and was free to spend the entire evening with Ned until it was time to join her friends at the motel. He tried his hand at deciphering the puzzle on the plaque but finally gave up.

"If you can solve this one, and keep out of trouble with Carla's pursuers and 'the cat', " he remarked, "you ought to get a vote of thanks from the Peruvian government!" Nancy laughed.

At ten o'clock she said goodbye to Hannah Gruen and her father. The housekeeper begged Nancy to be careful and the lawyer said, "No instructions from me, my dear, but you know that I wish you success and I'll be looking forward to your return."

When Nancy and Ned reached the airport motel, he carried her two bags into the lobby. One contained the plaque and Nancy said that she would carry that suitcase. "I'll check in the other one."

As Ned bade her goodbye and looked straight at her, Nancy detected a wistful look in his eyes. He said, "My thoughts are repetitions of your father's and Hannah's combined." He took both her hands in his and added, "You will come back safely, won't you?" He kissed her.

"I promise," Nancy answered, and waited until he drove off. Then a porter carried her bags to the room which she would share with Carla.

The Peruvian girl, as well as Bess and George, were already there. Bess teased Nancy. "I thought maybe you'd change your mind about going to Peru when Ned showed up."

Nancy smiled but did not reply, because at that moment the telephone rang.

Carla's heart sank. "Oh, somebody has found out where we are! Maybe El Gato!"

Nancy answered the phone, disguising her voice. A

man at the other end of the line said, "Police head-quarters calling. Is this Miss Drew? Chief McGinnis wants to talk to you."

Nancy did not admit who she was but merely said, "Please put him on."

The next instant Chief McGinnis's familiar voice said, "Nancy, I want you to come to headquarters immediately. It's very important."

· 3 ·

Strange Cancellation

WHEN Nancy told her companions about Chief McGinnis's request, George remarked, "Maybe they've caught Wallace."

Bess added, "I suppose you'll have to go to headquarters, Nancy. But how are you going to get there? We have no car."

"A taxi will do," Nancy replied. "Carla, I think you'd better come with me. After all, you know more about this case than I do."

The two girls reached police headquarters forty minutes later. Chief McGinnis had a prisoner brought into his office.

"Is this the man who came to your house and pretended to be a police detective?" the chief asked Nancy.

"Yes, he is."

Harry Wallace's eyes flashed. "I never saw this girl before in my life!" he shouted.

Nancy went on, "He tried to steal a valuable antique plaque. It belongs to this young lady." On purpose Nancy had not introduced Carla by name, hoping that perhaps the prisoner would give himself away by identifying her.

The man became sullen. "I'm not going to talk,"

he said. Turning to Chief McGinnis, he added, "You have no right to hold me. I haven't done anything wrong."

Again Nancy spoke up. "If you need any witnesses, Chief, I have two friends who were there at the time."

At this, Harry Wallace seemed to change his mind about talking. "Oh, all right," he said. "I didn't recognize Miss Drew at first. She looked different when I saw her."

Chief McGinnis stared at the prisoner hard. "Then you admit trying to steal the plaque?"

"No, I don't," Harry Wallace replied. "That plaque belongs to me!"

"What!" Carla cried out. "It does not!"

The prisoner made one more effort to clear himself. "I'm an importer in New York City. I buy articles from all over the world. That plaque was sold to me in South America. It was taken from my shop. Ever since then I've been trying to trace it. First I found out Miss Ponte here had it right in River Heights. And then I learned she gave it to Miss Drew."

There were faint smiles on the faces of Nancy and Chief McGinnis. The prisoner had indeed given himself away. The officer said, "I'm afraid, Mr Wallace, that you have tripped yourself up with your story. Now suppose you tell the truth."

The prisoner refused to say another word. Nancy whispered to Carla, "Is this the man who has followed you several times?"

"I think so, but I cannot be absolutely sure."

Nancy walked forward and whispered this information to the chief. She added, "Miss Ponte also received an anonymous warning note. Maybe Harry Wallace sent it. The note was in Spanish. Translated, it said, 'Beware of the cat.' Does that mean anything to you?"

Before answering, Chief McGinnis went to a bookcase and pulled out a loose-leaf ledger. He ran his fingers down the index, then turned to a page near the back of the book.

"Hmm!" he murmured, beckoning Nancy to take a look at the notation.

She leaned over his shoulder and read that there was a mysterious man in Peru who was known to the police there as El Gato. His name and whereabouts were not known, but he was listed as a "wanted person".

Chief McGinnis turned to the prisoner. "Things will go a lot easier with you if you tell us who El Gato is."

Startled, Harry Wallace jerked his shoulders uncomfortably and began to speak, then closed his lips tightly. After a few seconds he said, "You trying to pin something else on me? I don't know what you're talking about."

The officer ordered the prisoner taken away, telling him he could have a lawyer of his own choosing or the court would get one for him.

Wallace said, "I'll let you know tomorrow." He followed the guard out of the room.

Nancy and the chief discussed the case a few minutes longer, with Carla looking on wide-eyed. Finally she said, "Oh, I am so sorry to be such a lot of trouble."

Chief McGinnis gave her a fatherly smile. "We will probably end up thanking you for having the police of two continents looking for this mysterious El Gato. I hope, Nancy, that you solve the mystery of the crossword cipher and have time for some fun on your trip." He shook hands with both girls. Then they went back to their waiting taxi.

When they reached the motel, Bess and George were eager to hear what had happened. After Nancy and Carla had told of the episode at headquarters, George snorted, "If that Harry Wallace is an importer, then I'll bet a cookie he's a smuggler!"

Bess gave an involuntary shudder. "Already everything's getting complicated."

The following morning the girls had breakfast in their rooms, then hurried to the check-in counter at the airport. By noon they had arrived in New York City and went directly to the apartment of Nancy's aunt, Miss Eloise Drew. She was delighted to see them and happy to meet Carla. The four girls briefed her on the mystery and their plans.

"They sound very intriguing," Miss Drew commented. "Since you girls are going to Lima, you might be interested in the Peruvian exhibits here in New York. There are some at the Metropolitan Museum of Art, others at the Museum of Natural History and a special exhibit at the Gallery of Modern Art. On the other hand, perhaps Carla would prefer doing a little sightseeing in New York City."

"I think I would," she said. "I have seen very little of it and this city is such an exciting place."

Aunt Eloise had a suggestion. "Suppose I take Carla with me and you other girls go to the exhibits. They will give you a good idea of the history and customs of ancient Peru."

After luncheon Nancy, Bess and George set off. At the Metropolitan they were fortunate enough to join a group with a guide. During his lecture, he said, "The

Indians of ancient Peru, particularly the Incas, had a religion in which they worshipped the sun, thinking of it as a god.

"They also had a succession of human rulers, called the Inca, who were supposed to have received divine powers directly from the sun god. As you look at the exhibits, you will note that the decorations on many of them illustrate this fact."

The three girls were intrigued by the various effigies, most of them made of clay. Many were hunched-up figures, seated with their knees near their chins. "This was also the position in which they usually buried their mummies," the guide explained.

The young visitors stayed so long at the Metropolitan that they had time only to visit the special exhibit at the Gallery of Modern Art. Here all the ancient objects from Peru were gold. They included various kinds of jewellery. Many of the necklaces and earrings were studded with turquoise or other semiprecious stones.

"Goodness, what are those things over there?" Bess asked. "They look like golden Halloween masks."

The girls walked to the cases and read the cards on the wall behind these objects.

"Funerary masks," Nancy said.

A man standing nearby told them that the mask was not put over the mummy's face but laid down just above the head. "Nobody has found out why."

Suddenly George chuckled. "Look at that mask over there. It looks just like a llama's face. Do you suppose someone had it made for his pet llama that died?"

The man grinned. "Perhaps, or else for some important person who looked like a llama."

The object in the exhibit which interested Nancy most

was a large pair of hands and arms made of solid gold. The stranger explained that these were gauntlets, probably worn by a priest at a religious ceremony. The pieces had one imperfection—the fingernails were dark and corroded looking. "Those nails were made of silver," the man said. "They tarnished, then disintegrated."

Bess had been staring at one thumbnail which had not disintegrated. She remarked, "Some of the old Incas must have worn their nails mighty long."

Nancy glanced at her watch and told the other girls it was time to leave. They thanked the man for his help and hurried from the building.

When the girls reached the apartment house, Aunt Eloise and Carla had just arrived, so they all went up in the lift together. As Miss Drew unlocked her door, the telephone began to ring. She hastened to answer it.

"Oh, Hannah," she said. "It's good to hear from you. The girls got in all right and they're going to leave in a little while."

There was a pause, then she exclaimed, "What? You say the airline called and said the girls' flight has been cancelled?"

Nancy and her friends stared unbelievingly. Nancy went to the phone to talk to Hannah Gruen. The housekeeper reiterated what she had told Aunt Eloise.

"A man called from the airline to say your flight has been cancelled. He gave no reason but asked that I get in touch with you at once. I've been trying to do so for the past hour. You must have been out."

"Yes, we were," Nancy answered. "Oh, this is dreadful news!" She gave a sigh. "Well, we may be seeing you sooner than we expected."

After Nancy had put down the phone, she suddenly frowned. Finally she said to the others, "This might be a hoax. There's no reason to cancel a flight today. The weather's perfect. Something might have caused a delay, but not a cancellation. I'm going to call the airline and find out what's going on."

She spoke to the man at the ticket counter, then listened to his reply. Nancy said, "Thank you very much. We were told the flight had been cancelled. I'm glad it's not true."

Everyone was relieved to hear this, but they wondered who the man was who had phoned the Drews' house. Nancy said, "It couldn't have been Wallace, because he's in jail. He must have an accomplice."

"Someone," said Aunt Eloise, "doesn't want you to go to Peru. Maybe it's because he hoped to steal the plaque before you could leave the country with it."

Nancy had a determined look on her face. "Well, this time he's going to fail. But I'd like to know who he is."

When the girls said goodbye to Miss Drew, she begged them to take every precaution to avoid danger. They all promised and Nancy gave her aunt an extra hug of assurance.

It was late morning the next day when the great jet landed at the huge and attractive Lima airport. Bess exclaimed, "I can't believe I'm here, and so far from home so soon!"

As the girls went through the customs section, Carla caught sight of her parents through a glass partition. She blew them a kiss and then pointed out Señor and Señora Ponte to the other girls. They waved and smiled. Finally the baggage was cleared through customs and the group set off in the large family car.

Carla's parents proved to be delightful people. Both were tall, handsome brunettes. Señora and Carla resembled each other.

When they reached the residential section, the North American visitors were impressed by the large homes and beautiful gardens. The tree-shaded boulevards were wide and most of the lawns had tall iron fences round them.

The Pontes' own home was extremely attractive. Inside the front fence was a lovely garden. On one side stood a very old and gnarled evergreen tree which rose about twenty feet into the air. When Nancy admired it, Señor Ponte told her it was a *queñar*.

To the right of the path leading to the front door was a gilded life-size statue of an alpaca. "He's handsome!" Bess murmured.

Señor Ponte explained that it was a duplicate of a golden alpaca which originally had stood in the great square before the Temple to the Sun in the city of Cuzco. "I am sorry to say that when the Spanish conquistadors came and conquered the Incas, they demanded so much gold that their capital, Cuzco, was ruined. One of its ancient nicknames was 'The City of Gold'. "

A delicious luncheon was served in the beautifully furnished, Spanish-style dining room. Afterwards, Nancy unpacked the plaque and Carla explained what the girls had learned about it so far.

"That is very fine," Señora Ponte commended them

Carla and her mother, using Nancy's magnifying glass, pored over the indistinct markings of the cross-word cipher. Nancy, Bess and George listened to Señor Ponte's story about the plaque.

"It was lost in the family for several generations," he said. "Then, amazingly, the plaque was found among my grandfather's effects after he died. By this time it was in such worn condition that no one could decipher the message."

Nancy asked, "Do you think that perhaps many years ago someone did figure it out?"

"I do not think so, or else the story would have been known," he answered. "All we ever heard was that a young Inca Indian had come to the home of one of my ancestors and handed him the plaque. The Indian could not speak Spanish so they learned nothing from him. I presume he knew only the Quechua language used by the Incas."

The telephone rang and Señor Ponte excused himself. Bess remarked, "What a fascinating story!"

The others agreed.

Carla suggested that the visitors might like to see the rest of the house. The girls stood up and began to walk round, admiring the many art objects. The Pontes had exquisite old paintings from Spain, and several ornately carved chests and tables.

"This is like a museum," George remarked.

Finally the visitors returned to the living room. As they walked in with Señor Ponte, Carla was holding Nancy's magnifying glass. Suddenly she exclaimed:

"Oh, I think I have just figured out part of this mystery!"

· 4 ·

Curious Assistant

EVERYONE crowded round Carla as she pointed to the rest of the vertical line of letters.

"I think they spell *cola*. In Spanish that means tail."

Nancy's face broke into a broad grin. "Then the two words down are *mono cola*—monkey tail!"

"That's right." Señor Ponte nodded. "But what is the significance?"

No one could answer the question, but each was thinking hard.

"Probably," Bess suggested, "for some reason Señor Aguilar couldn't give the monkey a whole tail, so he carved the word 'tail'. "

"That sounds reasonable," Carla's father remarked.

"Maybe," said George, "this monkey had a special kind of tail. To find the answer, I suppose we'll have to consult books that tell about all sorts of simians. Do you have any such books?"

"I think so," Señora Ponte answered. "But I believe all monkeys have long tails. Only apes and baboons do not."

Her husband said, "Nancy, you haven't expressed an opinion. What do you think?"

The young sleuth replied slowly, "Since this plaque says monkey tail and part of the tail is cut off, I believe that fact is in itself some kind of clue to the mystery."

"You mean," Carla asked, "if we can figure out the significance of the tail, it will lead us to something valuable that our ancestor Aguilar hid or did in a secret place?"

"Yes, I do. I also think possibly the kind of wood the plaque is made of may have some bearing on the mystery. Do you know what kind of wood this is, Señor Ponte?" Nancy asked.

Carla's father shook his head. "To tell the truth, I never took the trouble to find out."

"Who could tell us?"

"The best person in Lima to ask is Señor Jorge Velez. He has a shop and factory and among other things he makes beautiful hand-worked wooden trays, plaques, bowls, salad forks and spoons. I am sure he will recognize what the plaque is made of. In any case, I know you girls will enjoy looking round his shop."

Carla's mother added, "You might like to make some purchases to take home."

Nancy was eager to visit the place at once. Señora Ponte said that the shop was not open at this hour. On Thursdays Señor Velez was there only between four and seven o'clock.

The plaque was wrapped carefully and the four girls set off just before four o'clock in Carla's sports car. She proved to be an excellent driver as she skilfully wound in and out among the heavy traffic of the business district until she came to Señor Velez's shop.

"It's a quaint old Spanish building," Bess remarked, admiring the rococo design above and around the heavy doorframe.

When the girls entered, two men were there arrang-

ing attractive polished bowls on shelves. One of the
men, who said he was the proprietor, was about fifty
years old. He had finely chiselled features and wore a
small moustache and a pointed beard. His hair, combed
straight back, was wavy and slightly long.

The girls introduced themselves. Señor Velez bowed
and said, "I am very happy to meet you."

He introduced the other man as Luis Llosa, his
assistant, who was about thirty years old. He was
surly looking, thin, dark, a bit stoop-shouldered and
had hairy arms. His eyes were shifty. Both men spoke
English.

Nancy unwrapped the plaque and showed it to
Señor Velez. "Can you tell us what kind of wood this
is made of?"

He examined the plaque carefully, even taking a
tiny sliver from the edge and holding it under a light.
Presently he said, "This is very old and very unusual.
The plaque is made of *arrayánes* wood. There is only one
place in the world where it is found."

"Here in Peru?" Carla asked.

Señor Velez shook his head. "It comes from a forest
of arrayánes trees at the end of a peninsula a good
distance from here. The place is in the Argentine."

"The Argentine!" Nancy exclaimed.

Secretly she had thought of going to the source of the
wood, hoping to find a clue there to the mystery. Now
the idea vanished.

"Exactly what part of the Argentine is it in?" Carla
asked Señor Velez.

The shop owner said that the peninsula stretched
into Lake Nahuel Huapi.

"If you girls could possibly manage it, you should

visit the arrayánes forest. It is thought that these trees are the descendants of prehistoric ones and are unlike any others on earth today.

"They are most unusual to look at. The place is a government preserve and nowadays no one is allowed to take any wood from there. I suppose that was not a rule when this plaque was made."

Carla began to tell Señor Velez about the mystery surrounding the object. As she was speaking, Nancy noticed that Luis Llosa had edged closer. He had a notebook in his hand and was making a sketch of the plaque. Somehow she did not trust this man, and when he reversed the plaque to the side with the cipher, she grabbed the ancient piece from him.

"This is private property," she told him firmly.

George, too, had noticed what the assistant was doing. With a lightening move she reached across the counter and grabbed the notebook. She tore out the page with the sketch on it, then laid the book back on the counter.

Luis Llosa glared at the girl, hatred in his eyes. He murmured something in Spanish under his breath, put the notebook into a pocket, and hastened into a back room.

There was silence until Señor Velez spoke. "Sometimes my assistant is over-curious," he said apologetically.

Nancy was embarrassed by the situation and quickly changed the subject. "Do you export your products to the United States?" she asked.

"Yes," the craftsman answered. "Many of them go to places in your country, especially to New York City."

On a hunch Nancy asked if he ever shipped anything to Harry Wallace.

"No, I think not. But let me look."

Señor Velez took an account book from a locked drawer in a desk and quickly turned to the W's. "Harry Wallace's name is not listed here," he said finally.

The girls looked over the handmade articles in the shop and made a few purchases, then left. When they reached the Pontes' home, Carla hung the plaque on the wall where it had always been before she had taken it to River Heights.

"From the time I was a tiny child, I always loved the monkey," Carla remarked. "By the way, do you girls feel like doing any more sight-seeing?"

Bess answered, "If you mean am I tired, I'm not."

The others were enthusiastic to see more of Lima and Nancy added, "I'm sure you have museums here. Do you think we might visit them and see if we can find some object with a monkey on it? It might give us a clue to why our monkey hasn't a whole tail."

Carla said that among the museums there were two in the city which specialized in pre-Columbian art objects.

"I believe one of them is closed at this hour, but I know the owner of the other one. He lives nearby and even if it's closed he will let us in. It's the Museo Rafael Larco Herrera."

When the girls arrived, they found the museum open and two other visitors there, a man and a woman. The man was a portly, red-faced North American. He was brandishing a cane to point out the various objects to the woman, apparently his wife.

She kept saying to him, "I can see the things. You

don't have to point out everything. You might knock one of these ancient figures off the shelf."

Each time she said this he looked at her with a supercilious smile. "Don't be so bossy. I know what I'm doing."

As the girls walked up and down the various aisles, marvelling at the hundreds of ancient bits of pottery, they watched intently for any which might have the design of a monkey on it.

There were jugs of all kinds, some plain, others shaped like animals or decorated with them.

Displayed in glass cases were many interesting pieces of jewellery. Presently Bess exclaimed, "Come here, girls! Did you ever see such huge earrings in your life?"

"They must weigh a ton," George remarked as she gazed at the huge discs of copper and turquoise.

As the girls went on, they could hear the voices of the couple not far ahead of them. The woman was still advising her husband not to keep pointing with his cane.

Nancy and her friends suppressed giggles. Carla, in the lead, entered another narrow passageway where the shelves on both sides were crowded with valuable, ancient pottery. The man and his wife stood gazing round. They did not seem to notice the girls' approach.

Suddenly Carla cried out, "I see a monkey jug!"

Nancy, directly behind her, stared at an upper shelf to which Carla was pointing. At the same instant, the man ahead of them suddenly swung his cane upward. The tip of it struck the monkey jug which teetered for a moment, then fell towards Carla's head.

The next second it would crash to the floor and be smashed to bits!

· 5 ·

A Perilous Ride

In a flash Nancy leaped forward and caught the falling monkey jug. Everyone breathed sighs of relief.

The first one to speak was the wife of the man who had swept the ancient artefact from the shelf with his cane. "What did I tell you, Charlie?" she half screamed. "That cane of yours will be the death of me!" She tried to take it from her husband but he held on tightly.

The fracas was stopped by a guard who had come on the run. Politely but firmly, he asked the couple to leave. "Charlie" suddenly looked subdued and followed his wife to the door.

After they had left, the girls burst into giggles. Bess remarked, "If I had a husband like that—"

"Or a wife like that—" George added.

Nancy was still holding the monkey jug. The guard reminded her that objects were not supposed to be removed from the shelves. Quickly George told him what had happened and the man praised Nancy for her fast action.

"*Gracias*," she said.

The others noticed that she had been turning the clay object round in her hands. The animal's head protruded from the front of the jug, but its tail was merely painted on.

41

"Do you get any clue from it?" Carla asked as Nancy set the ancient jug back on the shelf.

"Not really," the young sleuth answered, but she asked the guard if there were any significance to portraying monkeys with incomplete tails. He shrugged and said he had never heard of any.

The foursome finished their tour of the museum, then went home. While waiting for dinner, which is served late in South American households, Nancy and her friends sat down to talk with Carla and her parents.

After hearing what the girls had done that day, Señor Ponte asked Nancy, "Have you any ideas about how you will proceed with solving the mystery? What would you like to do next?"

Nancy's eyes sparkled and she said mischievously, "Oh, yes. I know what I'd like to do, but it's impossible."

"Nothing is impossible," said her host with a smile. "Tell me what is on your mind."

"A trip to the arrayánes forest."

At this announcement Bess and George blinked. Their friend was really reaching far!

To their surprise, Nancy's request did not seem to upset Señor Ponte one bit. Grinning, he told the girls that his company owned a private plane which was flying the next day into the Argentine.

"As a matter of fact, it will go very close to the peninsula where those unusual old trees are."

He went on to say that the executives of his company, including himself, were going to the beautiful Hotel Llao-Llao to attend a three-day conference and golf matches.

"The plane will fly to Bariloche and the group will

drive from there to the hotel. There is plenty of room in the plane for you four girls. How would you like to go?"

The visitors were almost speechless with delight, but finally Nancy said, "Oh, Señor Ponte, that would be marvellous! You say the arrayánes forest is not far from where we'll be staying?"

"The hotel is on the same lake and you can hire a boat for an excursion to the forest."

"Father," said Carla, hugging him, "you are a darling." As he looked startled at this unfamiliar remark, she added quickly, "That is what the girls up in River Heights say to people who do nice things."

Her father laughed and said, "I think we Peruvians should adopt the phrase. I like it."

Señor Ponte told the girls that the group from his company was leaving the following morning, so he advised his daughter and her friends to be ready early. He thought it might be a good idea for Nancy to take the plaque.

As Bess was preparing for bed, she remarked to George. "There's been so much excitement since we left home, I feel as if I will burst!"

George grinned. "Well, my dear fat cousin, that might be one way to lose some weight!"

The flight the following day was a delightful one over breathtaking scenery. Snow-capped mountains, a profusion of lakes, and verdant farmlands with hundreds of grazing cattle, stretched for miles and miles.

Bariloche was a quaint, interesting town. It had been settled by the Swiss, who had built everything to resemble the architecture in their homeland.

In less than half an hour the group arrived by car at

the Hotel Llao-Llao. It was a long rambling building in very attractive grounds and stood on a knoll overlooking the water.

In the centre of the hotel was a lobby and from this ran a wide corridor the full length of the building. There were shops along either side of one end. Directly ahead was a large lounge and a glassed-in porch overlooking the golf course.

Rooms on the first floor were assigned to the girls. A broad staircase led upwards. The girls walked instead of taking the lift.

Nancy and Clara's room overlooked the lake which stretched for miles and miles. Not far from the hotel was a dock where motor-boats could be hired.

"Look!" Bess exclaimed, pointing down to a roadway which led along the foot of the slope.

An ox was pulling a cart on which sat a sleepy-looking driver, holding the reins loosely.

"I want to take their picture," said Bess, and made a dash for her camera. By the time she had it set, the oxcart had moved round a bend and was lost to view.

"Better luck next time," George told her.

The girls unpacked and Nancy carefully laid the plaque in the bottom drawer of her bureau. Over it she put a crush-proof dress and a couple of sweaters.

George poked her head in the doorway. "Let's take a walk," she suggested. "This looks like an interesting place to explore."

"And we should make arrangements for someone to take us in a boat to the arrayánes forest tomorrow," Nancy added.

The girls changed into slacks, locked their doors, and hurried downstairs. Bess's camera swung from a

"Whoa! Whoa!" Nancy yelled

strap over her shoulder. "Maybe the oxcart will come back," she said hopefully.

First the girls went to the boat dock and made arrangements for the next day's trip. They were told there would be several other passengers.

"I hope it does not rain," the man said dolefully. "It looks as if it might."

"We'll go anyway," Nancy replied. "*Hasta la vista.* Be seeing you."

On the way back to the hotel the girls saw the oxcart parked at the side of the roadway, but the driver was not in sight. Bess decided this was a good chance to take the animal's picture. As she and the others approached the ox, they noticed a boy of about fourteen seated on the hillside nearby. A man was talking to him, but as soon as he saw the girls, the stranger hurried away.

"Hmm! He acts as if he's afraid of us!" George remarked.

Bess was about to snap a picture of the oxcart, when the boy rose from the embankment and said to Nancy, "You ride ox? You have picture taken on ox?"

As Nancy demurred, Bess said she thought this was a grand idea. "Please climb up. The picture will be a wonderful souvenir of our trip."

"Oh, all right," Nancy said.

With George's help she gave a little jump and landed squarely on the back of the ox. Instantly the boy, who was holding a stick in one hand, gave the animal a hard slap with it. The beast started off abruptly, nearly throwing Nancy to the ground.

She realized to her dismay that the ox had been

unhitched. She clung tightly to its neck, yelling, "Whoa! Whoa!" at the top of her lungs.

The other girls were aghast. They started running after the animal, which despite its size and clumsiness was making good speed.

Bess, though fearful, followed her cousin, who yelled, "We'll run up this hill and cut them off!"

She and George ran sideways up the slope, then down again several yards in front of the pounding animal.

"Do just what I do!" George commanded.

The two girls waved their arms wildly, crossing and uncrossing them. They spread their feet far apart and swayed from side to side. The ox, frightened by the gestures, pulled up short.

Nancy climbed down in a hurry. "Thanks, girls. Boy, what a ride! Bareback ox-riding isn't one of my favourite sports!"

"What do we do with this beast—leave him here?" George asked.

As if in answer to her question, the driver came running down the road. He spoke only a little English, but the girls gathered that he was blaming them for having unhitched the ox. They denied it vehemently, but wondered who had done so. Was it the boy? Or could it have been the man who had run off?

"We had better ask that boy," Carla suggested.

They walked back to the cart, but the lad was gone. When the driver arrived leading the ox, they told him about the boy and asked if he knew who he was.

"Maybe he from caddie house," the man said. "Name Tomás Rivero."

George was angry. "I think we should go to that

caddie house immediately and find out if the man we saw put Tomás up to that mean trick."

The others agreed and set off to find out. When they reached the caddie house, the master confirmed that the boy worked there. "Tomás left early today. He lives in Bariloche, but I'm afraid we don't have his address."

Nancy told the caddie master what had happened. "When Tomás comes again, will you please ask him about the man?" The caddie master agreed to do so, and the girls returned to the hotel.

When Nancy entered her room, she noticed that the bottom drawer of her bureau was slightly open. Knowing that she had closed it tightly, the young sleuth immediately became suspicious.

She fairly leaped across the room and yanked the drawer open. Nancy gasped in dismay!

· 6 ·

The Con Man

"WHAT's the matter?" George asked Nancy.

"The plaque! It's gone!"

A look of utter dismay spread across Carla's face. She said something in Spanish, then added in English, "What will we do? Now we can never solve the mystery! Oh, that monkey is what you say—a jinx."

The next moment she flung herself on a bed and began to weep. Bess threw her arms round the girl and tried to comfort her.

"We're all terribly sorry," she said. "But I'd like to bet Nancy will find the plaque."

"I'm certainly going to try," Nancy replied. "The first thing I shall do is go down to the desk and report the theft to the manager."

The clerk on duty took her into the manager's office where a pleasant-looking man, Señor Diaz, was in charge at the moment. Quickly Nancy told her story.

"I am very sorry to hear this," the man said. "The plaque sounds most unusual. It seems like a strange thing for anyone to steal. What would be the motive for such a theft?"

"I don't know," Nancy answered, "but the plaque has been in the Ponte family for hundreds of years and they will be greatly upset to learn it has been stolen."

"Miss Ponte is with you, is she not?" the man asked. "Does she know about this?"

Nancy nodded. "She is upstairs crying over the loss."

Señor Diaz tapped his desk with a pencil. "One thing is sure. Somebody with a key got into the room. This would indicate a chamber-maid or a porter. However, I assure you, Miss Drew, that I can vouch for the absolute honesty of all our employees."

Nancy said she doubted that the plaque would be of interest to them, anyway. More likely it had been stolen by an intruder with a skeleton key.

"Then it will be very hard to trace such a person," Señor Diaz said. He walked out to the lobby with Nancy. "I shall investigate the matter immediately. Can you give me any clues at all as to who the thief might have been?"

The young sleuth told him that in her home town of River Heights a man had tried to steal the plaque. "He claimed to be an importer in New York City." She also mentioned Luis Llosa, the craftman's assistant who had copied some of the markings on the plaque before he had been stopped.

Out of the corner of her eye, Nancy noticed a woman listening intently to the conversation. In a moment she approached the young detective and asked, "Is there a monkey on the plaque?"

Surprised, Nancy said, "Yes."

"I'm Mrs Smith," the woman said. "I have just come from one of the gift shops in the hotel. On the wall is a plaque with a monkey on it."

Nancy doubted that it could be Carla's property, but she thanked Mrs Smith and hurried towards the shop, with Señor Diaz following her.

As the two rushed in, Nancy stopped short. She could hardly believe her eyes. The plaque on the wall was indeed the valuable heirloom of the Ponte family!

She told this to Señor Diaz, and then asked the shop owner, Señora Violetta, how she had obtained the plaque.

"In a rather unusual way," the woman replied. "Less than half an hour ago one of the hotel's guests, Señor Manuel Sanchez, brought it in."

"But why did he bring it here?" Nancy asked, perplexed.

"To sell it," the shop owner answered. "Señor Sanchez said that he had brought the plaque to the hotel because he had had an order for this antique piece from a collector. The man was from the United States and was staying here. But when Señor Sanchez arrived, the buyer had already left."

Nancy was intrigued by this series of falsehoods and encouraged the shop owner to go on.

The woman smiled and asked, "First, would you mind telling me, señorita, why you are so interested?"

"Because," Nancy replied, "this plaque belongs to a friend of mine and was stolen."

Señora Violetta gasped. "Oh dear, oh dear!" she exclaimed. "I have done something dreadful!"

"Please tell the whole story," Señor Diaz urged.

A frightened look had come over the woman's face, but she went on, "Señor Sanchez told me that he did not want to bother taking the plaque all the way home. He wondered if I would be interested in buying it."

"And you did?" Nancy asked.

The shop owner shook her head. "At the time Señor Sanchez was here a customer walked in. She is an avid antique collector and recognized the plaque as a valuable curio.

"Hearing that he wanted to sell the plaque, she asked him how much he wanted for it. When he said a hundred and fifty dollars, she bought it and gave him cash. In turn she handed me ten dollars as my commission."

Señor Diaz asked why the customer had not taken the plaque with her.

"She did not want to bother carrying the plaque up to her room just then," Señora Violetta replied, "and asked me to keep it overnight."

Nancy asked what Manuel Sanchez looked like. The woman described the man as having red hair and small features, and wearing a black-and-white checked sports jacket.

At once a thought came to Nancy. The man she had seen talking to the caddie had worn a black-and-white checked coat! His hat had been pulled down so far, she had not noticed the colour of his hair. It was quite possible he had unhitched the ox, and bribed the boy to slap the beast with a stick if Nancy or one of the other girls should get on its back.

"A runaway or an accident would keep us from our rooms for some time," Nancy thought. "This would give Sanchez a chance to go to my bedroom. He let himself in with a skeleton key, hunted for the plaque and took it."

Nancy figured that he probably had quickly made detailed drawings or even taken photographs of the plaque. Then, worried about an alarm over the theft, he felt it best to get rid of the stolen property.

"Pretty clever of him to have thought of the gift

shop," Nancy said to herself. "And what a surprise he's in for when the management questions him."

She said to Señor Diaz, "What is the number of Señor Sanchez's room? You're going to have him arrested at once, aren't you?"

The man nodded vigorously. As he went to the desk to look in the guest register, Señora Violetta handed Nancy the plaque.

"I am sure your friend will be relieved to see this. And I certainly hope the police can get back my customer's hundred and fifty dollars."

"I hope so too," said Nancy, and hurried off.

When she reached the desk, Señor Diaz had just finished checking the guest list. He turned to Nancy and said in a worried voice, "No Manuel Sanchez has been registered here."

Nancy panicked. The thief had vanished and no doubt had all the necessary information to solve the mystery of the crossword cipher before she could do so!

The young sleuth climbed the staircase and was calm again by the time she opened the door to her bedroom. "Good news!" she cried out happily, and presented the plaque to the tear-stained Carla.

"Oh, Nancy, where did you find it?"

Nancy quickly related the story and told of her worry about Manuel Sanchez having all the information he wanted. "He must be an accomplice of Luis Llosa and Harry Wallace."

George said with determination, "Let's see to it that we beat that gang at their own game!"

Just before dinnertime two police officers arrived to question Carla and the other girls, as well as the shop owner. They had also notified the woman who had purchased the plaque from Sanchez, and reported that she was very angry about the whole affair. She was demanding that the hotel give her back the hundred and fifty dollars she had spent.

"Of course you are not concerned in that part of the case," one of the officers told the girls. "We will let you know if we apprehend Sanchez. Can you tell us anything that might help solve this mystery?"

Nancy revealed her suspicions that there might be a liaison between Sanchez and Luis Llosa. She also mentioned that the two possibly had some connection with Harry Wallace of New York because of their interest in the plaque. The officers thanked her and left. No word came from the police that night or early the next morning, and Carla was discouraged.

Trying to be cheerful, Bess said, "That horrible Sanchez is probably thousands of miles from here by now. And good riddance. Then he won't bother us again." All the girls began to feel a sense of relief.

Nancy decided to take the plaque to the arrayánes forest and show the carvings to the warden there. She might get a clue from him!

At ten o'clock the four friends went aboard the launch. It had a cabin to accommodate about twenty people and an open aft deck. The pilot's compartment, which opened directly from the cabin, was reached by a short ladder. The day was cloudy and cool, with beautiful clouds scudding across the sky.

The crowd on board was jolly and the girls soon became acquainted with a delightful couple from England. The husband was a camera enthusiast like Bess, and the two snapped picture after picture of the many snow-capped mountains on either side of the lake.

After the launch had been cruising for about half an hour, it began to slow down. Finally the engines stopped. After a long wait the pilot left his seat and came to call back into the cabin. "*Sin gasolina*," he announced.

"No fuel!" several of the Americans exclaimed, and Carla added, "What will we do?"

A broad grin came over the pilot's face. He rattled off something in Spanish. Carla turned to the girls and translated.

"He said, 'Who would like to swim to shore for help?'"

·7·

Another Challenge

AT the pilot's facetious request, many of the passengers
in the cabin of the launch began to laugh. Others were
angry that they were stranded in the middle of Lake
Nahuel Huapi.

"There is no excuse for this," said one woman.

"We may have a long, long wait before help comes!"
another burst out.

Although Nancy said nothing, inside she was fuming
with impatience and thinking, "This is the only boat
going to the arrayánes forest today. If it doesn't run,
we'll never be able to make the trip, because we have to
fly back to Lima tomorrow."

George was mumbling, "We may miss an important
clue to solving the mystery of the crossword cipher."

The Englishman, with whom the girls had made
friends, suddenly stood up. He walked forward and
climbed the ladder into the pilot's compartment. His
wife, Mrs Horace, told the girls that he was an engineer.
She said he thought something other than lack of fuel
might be the trouble with the launch.

"Oh, I hope he's right," said Bess.

"And I hope he can fix it," George added.

Carla sighed. "From the very beginning of this case
we have had nothing but setbacks," she said dolefully.

Nancy patted her friend's hand. "We'll get out of this."

Presently the engineer called to Carla, asking her to come to the pilot's cabin. "This man speaks very little English," he said. "Would you mind translating for me?"

Carla said she would be glad to do so and rapidly told the pilot that the Englishman was an engineer and would like to make an inspection of the engines. The pilot shrugged and told him to go ahead. The engine room was under the pilot's compartment. A door led below.

It began to rain and people who had been on the aft deck crowded into the cabin. They asked what was causing the delay.

"I wish we knew," Mrs Horace replied.

Nancy and her friends watched as Mr Horace examined wires and pipes. Presently he requested Carla to translate for him again.

"Tell the pilot that I'm sure the launch is not out of fuel. I think the fuel line is clogged. Can he clean it out himself?"

When the skipper heard this, a broad grin crossed his face and he said rapidly, "Yes, I can clean it."

At once he went to work. Shortly, the passengers were relieved to hear the engines sputter, then start up with a steady throb.

"*Olé!*" cried the Spanish passengers.

"Yeah!" the English-speaking ones shouted.

The first stop on the trip was Victoria Island. Here the tourists climbed a hill to a delightful hotel, where they had a tasty lunch which included huge slices of home-made bread.

As Bess reached for her third piece, George grabbed her cousin's arm. "No you don't!" she said.

Meekly Bess put the slice of bread back into the basket and finished her salad. Soon after lunch, the travellers assembled at the dock and once more started off. The rain had slackened to a drizzle and by the time they reached the peninsula the sun was shining.

"Doesn't the forest look enchanting?" Bess said, gazing towards the pinkish-yellow growth of trees ahead.

The girls hurried from the dock, but before entering the forest, stopped to examine a large round plaque nailed to a tree.

"Oh, could this be a clue?" Carla asked excitedly.

The circular piece of arrayánes wood was a little bigger than the Pontes' plaque. There was an inscription on it which Carla translated:

" '*Trees are man's good friends. Do not wound them.*' "

"How poetic!" Bess murmured.

As the girls skirted the beach, which was covered by loose rocks and stones of various sizes, they looked intently into the most amazing woods they had ever seen.

"It's like a fairyland!" said Nancy.

The enormously high trees grew straight up, but not as single units. Several trunks rose from a common base and each one in turn had more upward branching limbs.

The trees had no bark. George ran her hand over the wood. "Umm, smooth as satin."

"It's the colour of evergreen wood," Nancy said, "but these trees don't have needles." She gazed at the thick, small-leafed foliage which grew high overhead.

"It's so peaceful in here!" Bess murmured as she

stepped over a tree root which had grown above ground. It trailed for some distance, then disappeared into the ground near another tree. "How strange!"

One of the tourists near her, who had overheard the conversation, said, "I understand that these roots run a long way and start forming a new tree. Probably there's a network of roots under this forest."

Nancy gazed all around. "Actually," she said, "these so-called trees are more like gigantic bushes. Maybe they once *were* bushes for Diplodocuses to feed on."

"Diplo-who?" Bess asked.

"Plant-eating dinosaurs," Nancy explained with a smile.

George grinned. "Can't you just see one of them rubbing himself on this nice smooth bark and reaching up to eat the leaves? But tell me, did they have those monsters in South America as well as North America?"

Nancy laughed. "You can't prove anything by me," she said.

Presently the girls passed a small attractive log cabin where they assumed the warden of this government preserve lived. Nancy suggested that on the way back they stop and talk to him.

Some twenty minutes later they rapped on the cabin door. It was opened by a pleasant middle-aged man. When Nancy told him she would like to ask a few questions about the forest, he invited the girls inside. They introduced themselves and the warden said, "My name is Romero. What can I tell you?"

Nancy took Carla's plaque from its wrapping and showed it to him.

He examined the curio with interest. "This is very

old. Too bad the markings aren't plainer. Have you any idea what they mean?"

"No, and that's why I brought it along to show you. We understand it is made of arrayánes wood and is about three hundred years old. Have you any records here to show who might have been in this vicinity at that time?"

Romero shook his head. "I imagine it was pretty wild, but whether or not anybody ever lived here I have never heard."

Carla said she had an ancient ancestor by the name of Aguilar who presumably had carved the plaque. "No one has ever figured out its significance, but now we girls are trying to do so."

The warden showed interest and asked if she could tell him any more about her ancestor.

"He was supposed to have been an excellent artist and an adventurer," Carla replied. "I suppose he travelled around a great deal."

Romero said that he knew of one person who might possibly help the girls. "But he does not live round here. He is an old man—a full-blooded Inca Indian who lives in Cuzco, Peru. He knows more stories and legends about the history of all of South America than anybody I have ever heard of."

Nancy realized that Cuzco was many miles from Lima. Could this Indian offer enough help to make a trip there worth while?

As if in answer to her unspoken question, Romero went on, "Even if Maponhni cannot help you with your mystery, you girls should visit Cuzco while you are in South America. Some of the original walls of the ruined city are still standing and nearby there are several other great ruins—a fortress, in particular."

"I'd love to see it and also meet Maponhni," said Nancy. "I have a hunch he can help us."

The warden said he knew the old Indian would be glad to see them. With a twinkle in his eyes, Romero added, "Maponhni will probably say to you, '*Munanki! Imaynan caskianqui?*' "

"That is not Spanish," Carla said. "What does it mean?"

Romera laughed. "It is the old Inca language, Quechua. It means, 'Hello! How are you?' "

The girls repeated the phrase several times, then Nancy asked how they should reply.

"You will say, '*Hucclla, yusul paiki.*' "

The visitors groaned. "I'll never be able to learn that," Bess declared. "What does it mean?"

"It means, 'Good, thank you,' and *Cutimunaikicama* means 'Goodbye.' "

While Nancy and Carla were trying to memorize the three phrases, George walked round the cabin. On one wall she noticed a bunch of knotted strings of various colours tied together and suspended from several nails. She asked what it was.

"That is called a *quipu*," Romero said. "It was the way the old Incas kept records. They did not have a written language or a way of counting. I will show you how this works."

He explained that the different coloured cords stood for various things. "For instance, a red string could indicate the king and the knots on that particular string might indicate how many wives and children he had. The old Inca rulers and their nobles were polygamists."

"But the common people weren't?"

"No. Each labourer, called a *puric*, was allowed only one wife."

George reached up and counted the knots, some of which were single, others doubled or in groups. "It would be beyond me," she said, "to figure this out. I guess that old king had a mighty big family."

The warden told the girls that scholars were still working on the puzzle of the quipu. If they could learn the meaning of the knots, they might discover some of the history of the Incas which was not yet known.

At that moment the girls heard a boat horn and knew they were being summoned to the launch. They thanked the warden for the interesting visit and said they must hurry off.

As they were leaving, Romero said, "While you are in Cuzco, be sure to go on to Machu Picchu. That is even more of a mystery than Cuzco. Nobody knows what it looked like when it was a city. That is another puzzle for you to solve, Miss Drew."

Nancy smiled. "Another challenge!" she said gaily.

Bess groaned. "Nancy, you have enough challenges already."

The girls said goodbye to the warden and hurried off through the forest. The launch's horn sounded again.

As they approached the beach, George suddenly pointed ahead and shouted, "Look out, everybody!"

Hurtling towards them was a large stone! As they ducked, the rock whizzed overhead and hit a tree with a resounding thud.

The next moment it ricocheted and struck Nancy a stinging blow on the back. Stunned, she teetered for a moment, then toppled over!

·8·

Spanish Disguise

FORTUNATELY, Nancy was not unconscious. She admitted to feeling woozy, but declared she would be all right in a little while. Carla said she would run ahead and ask the pilot to wait.

"Tell him I'll be there in a few minutes," Nancy called. She managed a wan smile. "We wouldn't want to be left here."

George, having made sure that Nancy was not badly hurt, dashed down a slight slope to the beach. Hoping to spot the person who had thrown the rock, she looked up and down. No one was in sight.

"Maybe he's hiding," George said to herself. "I'll hide too, and if he thinks we've all gone, he may come out." She grinned. "I'll use a little judo on him!"

George slipped behind a big arrayánes tree at the edge of the beach and waited. No one appeared, but presently she heard a motor being revved up. She stepped from hiding to see who was in the approaching boat.

Two men were pulling out of a small cove in a motor-boat. Their backs were turned to George, but she instantly guessed that one of them was Manuel Sanchez. He had red hair and wore a black-and-white checked sports jacket.

"I'll bet I did pick up a clue after all," George thought as she climbed up the slope to rejoin her friends. Carla had returned and she and Bess were just helping Nancy to her feet.

"Did you find out anything?" Carla asked George.

"I think so."

When she told about the man with the red hair and black-and-white sports jacket, the others agreed that he probably was Sanchez.

Bess expressed her worries. "Nancy, that man is determined to injure you. Oh, why don't the police catch him?"

"I'm sure they will," Nancy said quietly.

The girls walked slowly to the launch, where the pilot and Mr and Mrs Horace expressed concern over Nancy's accident.

"I'm glad it was no worse," the woman added.

The girls said nothing about whom they suspected of having thrown the rock. But they would certainly tell the police.

The pilot made a stop at Victoria Island again, where, he said, his passengers could spend an hour or two. The girls immediately went up to the hotel and engaged a room. They had tea served, and Carla got in touch with the police. As soon as Nancy had finished her tea, the others insisted that she crawl into the bed.

"And go to sleep," Bess ordered.

Nancy was only too glad to do this and within seconds was sound asleep. The others tiptoed out and waited on the ground floor until ten minutes before sailing time. Then they wakened her.

"That was just what I needed," Nancy declared. "I've completely recovered."

When they returned to the Hotel Llao-Llao, Nancy sought out Señor Diaz and asked if there had been any report on Manuel Sanchez or the caddie responsible for the runaway incident.

"I have heard nothing," he replied. "I am sorry."

As it neared dinner-time, Nancy said to the other girls, "I must confess I don't feel like going to the dining room. If you'll all excuse me, I'll have supper in my room and get to bed early."

George grinned. "That's the most sensible thing I've heard you say in a long time. You do just that."

"Carla can dress in George's and my room," Bess said.

Carla gathered up some clothes and they said good night to Nancy. The three girls dressed and went downstairs to dinner. On the way to their assigned table, they passed a long one filled with men. Mr Ponte was among them and as an official of the company was seated at the head.

"Are you all having a good time?" he asked the girls. "And where's Nancy?"

The trio hesitated to tell him what had happened. Finally George spoke up. "Nancy doesn't give up easily, but she confessed to being very tired."

Carla added, "She is going to have dinner in her room and go to bed early."

"That is probably a good idea. Well, have fun on the rest of your stay here and I shall see you tomorrow for our trip back."

The girls went on to their table. Here they learned from the waiter that the first course would be smörgåsbord.

When Carla saw all the food on display, she exclaimed

over the quantity. "If I take even one little titbit of each of these delicious things, I will never eat any more dinner!"

The girls began to help themselves. Carla and George did not fill their plates, but Bess took three kinds of fish, chicken salad, vegetable salad and half a melon.

The others teased her, but she ignored them. When Bess was served a large dish of cream soup, followed by a main course of roast beef, potatoes and vegetable, as well as dessert—a rich cake topped with ice cream—she began to falter.

"Oh, I know I'm going to burst!" she said, after swallowing the last mouthful of dessert.

George looked at her cousin disapprovingly. "If you have a tummy-ache tonight, enjoy it by yourself!" Bess was silent.

After dinner the girls wandered into the lounge and sat down to talk.

Carla was quiet for a while, then she said, "I have been trying to think of some way I could help Nancy solve the mystery and I have just had what you call a brainstorm. Tell me if you think I am crazy to try it."

Carla outlined a plan she had in mind. In one of the gift shops she would buy a large Spanish shawl and a fan.

"I have a dress with me that is like a Spanish dancer's," she whispered. "I could fix myself up to look like an entertainer and in that costume I could try to locate Manuel Sanchez."

"How?" Bess and George asked.

"In the basement of this hotel," Carla explained, "there is a very large casino where various games are played. It is not run by the hotel and is open to anyone who wants to come and play."

"Yes?" Bess prompted as Carla paused.

"It is possible that Manuel Sanchez will come there. If I can play my part right, so he does not recognize me, I might be able to talk with him and learn something worth while."

"And turn him over to the police, I hope," George declared.

"Of course."

Bess remarked that the scheme sounded very risky, but George was inclined to think that it might work. "We'd better keep an eye on you, though. Bess can take the first watch and I'll take the second."

Carla agreed to this protection and went off to purchase a shawl and a fan. The other two girls went up to their room.

When Carla arrived with her purchases, Bess said, "I hope Nancy's asleep so you can tiptoe in and bring your bag across the hall to our room without her hearing you."

Carla was able to accomplish this quietly.

"I think it would be best if I changed my clothes in the ground-floor powder room," Carla told Bess and George. "Then no one will recognize me as the same girl who went in. I will put this Spanish dress in a shopping bag with these other things. Bess, when you come down to follow me, do not speak. Pretend you never saw me before."

"All right. How much time do you want?"

Carla said ten minutes would do. Bess waited exactly ten minutes, then walked down the stairs. She stopped to look in various shop windows along the corridor.

Presently Carla emerged from the powder room and Bess could not help gasping in amazement. "What a transformation!" she thought.

The Peruvian girl looked utterly bewitching. Her hair was piled high on her head and a tall Spanish comb at the back completed the coiffure. Over it all was a beautiful black lace shawl which hung in a point down the back, almost to the bottom of Carla's gay Spanish dress. The other two ends of the shawl were shorter and lay gracefully on her shoulders.

Carla's eyebrows had been heavily darkened. She had attached long, curling black lashes which gave her a flirtatious look. The "Spanish dancer" seemed about ten years older and very sophisticated.

"Oh, oh!" Bess thought. "I'd really better keep an eye on Carla or this Spanish beauty will be kidnapped by some dashing cavalier!"

Carla walked up the hall, a black-beaded purse held nonchalantly in one hand. Reaching the door which led to the casino, she opened it and started down the staircase. Bess had turned and followed at what she considered an unobtrusive distance.

At the foot of the stairs, the girls showed free admission passes which Carla had obtained earlier from the desk, after revealing her plan to Señor Diaz.

The brightly lighted casino was filled with men and women, most of them at the gaming tables, others just milling around. Everyone stopped to look at Carla and she received many invitations to come and play the games.

To each one she replied, "Thank you, no. I am looking for Señor Manuel Sanchez. Have you seen him?"

Person after person said No. But finally a dark-haired man, who extended the same invitation and received the same reply, said:

"*Olé!* Sanchez did not tell me he had a date with such a gorgeous girl."

Bess was surprised that the man had replied in English. He went on, "My friend Sanchez could not come tonight—he hurt his arm this afternoon."

Bess's heart began to pound. Manuel Sanchez had probably injured himself when he had thrown the rock at Nancy!

The dark-haired stranger said to Carla, "If you wish, I will take you to Sanchez and his sister."

Bess was suspicious of the man. On the other hand, he might not be involved in Sanchez's crooked schemes. In any case, she hoped Carla would not accept. To her dismay, the Peruvian girl said she would be happy to go along.

"Where is Señor Sanchez?" Carla asked.

"You will soon find out," the dark-haired man replied. "Come with me."

He led Carla out of a side door of the casino and headed through the hotel grounds for the shore. Bess was extremely worried. She followed along the path as closely as she dared, wishing George were with her.

The stranger led the way directly to the dock, where a motor-boat rocked gently on the water. He took hold of Carla's arm to help her into it, but at this point she refused to go. He held on.

"Get on board!" the dark-haired man said firmly. "You are no friend of Sanchez, but I am going to find out who you are!"

As Carla struggled to free herself, Bess screamed loudly and ran forward.

·9·

Wooden Clue

As Bess continued to scream loudly, the man who was endeavouring to abduct Carla let go of her. He jumped into the waiting motor-boat.

Bess noticed for the first time that there was a pilot, but it was too dark for her to see his features. The craft roared off.

"Oh, Carla!" she cried out, running forward to her friend. "Did he hurt you?"

"He pinched my arm pretty hard, but other than that I am all right," Carla answered.

Her Spanish costume was askew and her hair dishevelled. As the two girls turned to walk back to the hotel, they were amazed to see people running from various directions.

"Who screamed? Who got hurt?" a man asked.

Bess tried to explain in English and Carla in Spanish.

"Where did those men go? I will get them!" said a young man.

Bess pointed down the lake. The motor-boat was already out of sight. "It's hopeless," she said.

By this time one of the hotel porters had pushed his way through the group and asked who the men were.

"We don't know," Bess replied. Then, on a hunch, she added, "Did you see a man around the hotel who had red hair and wore a black-and-white checked sports jacket?"

"Yes, I did. It was yesterday. He was on the second floor. I do not know him." Suddenly the porter recognized Bess. "The man you speak of stood by the door across the hall from you."

"What was he doing?" Carla asked.

"Nothing when I passed by."

After a few more questions and answers, the girls learned that the stranger had been there about the time the plaque must have been stolen. The porter also said that later the same red-haired person had been met on the grounds of the hotel by a man who lived in Bariloche.

"Do you know this man's name?" Bess asked excitedly.

"It is Frederic Wagner. He owns a motor-boat and he might have taken the red-haired man."

Bess and Carla looked questioningly at each other. Both had the same thought. Was the pilot of the kidnapper's motor-boat this same Frederic Wagner? And was he perhaps the one who had taken Sanchez away from the arrayánes forest?

The crowd dispersed, assured of the girls' well-being. Bess and Carla returned to the hotel. They found Nancy awake and George talking to her. As Carla took off her Spanish costume, Bess told the story of what had happened.

Nancy sat straight up in bed. She reached for the telephone directory on the bedside table and began to riffle the pages. Presently she said, "Here it is. Frederic Wagner in Bariloche."

George asked what she planned to do with the

information. "Call Señor Diaz and suggest he get in touch with the police immediately. This is too good a lead not to follow up."

Nancy spoke to Señor Diaz, who promised to pass along the information to the authorities at once.

"Miss Drew, you are a fast-working detective," he praised her.

Nancy laughed. "I have some excellent assistants. And this time all the credit goes to two of them, Misses Bess Marvin and Carla Ponte."

"Well, congratulate them for me," Señor Diaz said. "And now I'll telephone the police."

The girls hoped that they would get some word later that evening, but none came.

Nancy sighed. "I have a strong hunch that Sanchez is hiding out with Wagner, but after what happened, they probably didn't go back to his home. The police will have to wait until they show up there."

At seven the next morning Nancy's telephone rang and she jumped to answer it. The Bariloche police were calling.

"Is this Miss Drew?"

"Yes."

"We have two men in custody. One is Frederic Wagner. The other refuses to give his name, but we think it is Manuel Sanchez."

The speaker requested that the girls come to Bariloche headquarters as soon as possible and bring the owner of the shop where the plaque transaction took place.

"I'll inquire where she lives and we'll all come together," Nancy promised.

The clerk at the desk said that the shop was not open on Sunday, but he offered to call the woman at home and let Nancy talk with her. The gift-shop owner was delighted to hear that the police had a suspect in custody and readily agreed to go with the girls.

"I have a car. Suppose I pick you up at eight-thirty."

"Thank you very much," said Nancy. "We'll be ready."

The four girls dressed quickly and went downstairs to have breakfast. By eight-thirty they were at the driveway entrance to the hotel. Señora Violetta drove up and the girls hopped in. She was aghast upon hearing what had happened to Carla the night before.

"You were very brave to undertake such detective work," she said.

"I must admit I was very scared," Carla replied.

When the group reached police headquarters, the two prisoners were brought in to Chief Castro's office.

Señora Violetta pointed to Sanchez and cried, "He is the man! He is the one who sold the stolen plaque!"

The police chief turned to the shop owner and the girls. Pointing to the other prisoner, he asked, "Do you recognize this man?"

All of them said they did not.

"He is Frederic Wagner," the chief said. "Unless you wish to file a complaint against this man, we cannot hold him."

At that moment a policeman walked into the room and spoke to his superior. After a few moments' conversation, Chief Castro said:

"A quantity of arrayánes wood has been found in your home, Señor Wagner. You know it is scarce and against the law to remove any from that special forest."

Wagner murmured, "I didn't get the wood from there. I got it—somewhere else."

"Suppose you tell us where." But Wagner refused to do this.

"We will hold you until you talk," the chief said. He turned to Señora Violetta and the girls. "We will take full statements from all of you."

Nancy gave details of the runaway ox and her suspicion that Sanchez was the instigator of the near accident.

Carla told about the plaque being stolen from her bedroom, and of the attempted abduction. "I think Wagner was the pilot of the boat and the kidnapper is a friend of his and Manuel Sanchez."

Chief Castro smiled. "You girls have had a rough time during your stay in the Argentine. Do visit our country some time to have fun!"

"I'd like to," Nancy answered, and the other girls nodded.

Señora Violetta took the girls to a church service, then back to the hotel. As they walked into the lobby, Señor Diaz hurried to them with a woman whom he introduced as Mrs Percy—the one who had paid the hundred and fifty dollars for the plaque. She was overjoyed to hear the good news.

"I suggest," said Nancy, "that you go to headquarters at Bariloche and put in a claim for your money."

"I will certainly do that and thank you very much," Mrs Percy said. She smiled. "You know I fell in love with that funny monkey. I am sorry to lose him."

Nancy and her friends went upstairs to pack. While Clara was folding clothes into her suitcase, she brought up the subject of the arrayánes wood which had been found in Wagner's home. "What do you think he uses it for?"

"I wish I knew," Nancy replied. "maybe the police here will be able to find out. I'm glad anyway, that we still have the plaque."

"And that all of us are in one piece!" George added.

Carla sighed. "This whole thing is so complicated. When I asked you, Nancy, to work on my monkey mystery, I had no idea it would turn out to have so many angles to it."

Nancy laughed. "I didn't, either. But the more complicated the mystery is, the more fun it is to solve."

Soon after lunch, Señor Ponte came for his daughter and her friends. Together, they drove to the Bariloche airport where the rest of his group was waiting. The men were busy talking business and discussing the golf matches.

When Carla learned that her father had won the big trophy, she hugged him. "Father, that is wonderful! Congratulations!"

The other girls congratulated him too. After some urging, he opened one of his bags and showed them a silver cup. His company awarded it each year to the best golfer at the Llao-Llao event.

Everyone boarded the plane and their bags were put behind the luggage harness just aft of the pilots' open compartment. As soon as clearance came from the tower, the pilot took off.

For a long time Nancy sat mulling over various angles of the mysteries. But presently she became restless and decided to walk forward for a little exercise.

When she reached the passenger-loading door, located just behind the crew's compartment, Nancy

Nancy felt herself being sucked out of the plane

paused and stood gazing with interest at the pilot and co-pilot. She marvelled at the huge bank of switches, lights, buttons and dials that almost surrounded the men. The plane was flying high now and at cruising speed.

Suddenly, without warning, the door near Nancy began to open. The next instant it swung up and outward. She felt herself being sucked out of the plane!

Nancy made a wild grab for the luggage harness and clung tightly, but it seemed as if she did not have strength enough against the terrific wind to grasp it very long. She froze in terror.

Others in the plane had been reading, but in an instant they felt a rush of air and looked up. All were horrified when they saw Nancy's predicament.

Señor Ponte and a companion jumped up and grabbed Nancy. But they in turn felt themselves being pulled towards the opening! Two men rushed forward and helped to pull all three to safety. Nancy dropped into an empty seat. She began to feel very dizzy.

By this time the crew had been alerted. The co-pilot leaped out of his seat and started back to see about closing the door. But at that moment it ripped off. Then a loud *thump* resounded from the rear of the fuselage. The plane shuddered violently.

"What is going on?" the captain shouted to his co-pilot.

"The door! It's ripped off the fuselage!"

"It must have struck the stabilizer!" the captain concluded. "We have tail damage! But we still have some control left!"

The pilot ordered his passengers to don their oxygen masks and fasten their seat belts immediately. They quickly obeyed. After Nancy had taken several whiffs of oxygen, the dizziness left her and she was able to breathe normally.

Now a new worry took hold of the passengers. The plane began to yaw. Everyone sat tense and nervous.

In as steady a voice as he could muster, the pilot said, "I will try to make it to Lima."

10

The Shuttered Balcony

GRIM-FACED, the passengers clutched their seat arms as the pilot dived to a lower altitude. Still the damaged plane rolled and tossed.

Nancy glanced at the open doorway and closed her eyes. She felt ill, still shocked from her narrow escape. She realized that everyone in the plane was in grave danger and never took her eyes from the pilot.

"He's marvellous," she thought as he managed to hold the swaying craft on course.

The passengers were swung from side to side, then forward and backward. But the sturdy plane kept on for miles and miles.

Finally it began a descending turn.

"You can take off your oxygen masks now!" the pilot announced. "We will be back on the ground in a few minutes. I have radioed the control tower to give us immediate clearance to land."

The yawing became increasingly worse as the craft neared the runway. With great effort the pilot manoeuvred into position and at last touched down. The plane bounced into the air, then settled again. A crash tender and an ambulance followed the plane as it taxied towards the parking ramp.

A sense of relief settled over Nancy. Everyone was

safe! Carla had told her how carefully the planes of Señor Ponte's company were inspected, so Nancy was sure that the door had been tampered with. She felt personally responsible.

"I'm the one who's trying to solve a mystery which several other persons definitely don't want me to solve," she thought ruefully. "If I hadn't taken this case, the near accident probably would have been avoided.

"But I mustn't think about this any more," the young sleuth told herself. "We're safe and I should be thankful for that."

When the plane rolled to a stop Nancy noticed that a crowd of people were waiting for it. As the passengers unfastened their seat belts, they all praised the pilot. The young man brushed it off with a shy smile.

"Flights like that keep me from getting bored with my job," the pilot said jokingly. Then he added soberly, "But now I want to find out why that door came off."

When Nancy started to get up, she felt as if her legs were made of rubber. At the same moment Bess remarked that she felt wobbly, adding, "I never want to go through such a thing again! Oh, Nancy, to think we almost lost you!" Tears filled Bess's eyes.

George and Carla hugged Nancy. They said little, but their expressions revealed what was in their hearts.

The stairway was rolled up to the door and the passengers descended to the field. All round them, men were talking excitedly in Spanish. Mechanics hurried to the top of the steps, and examined the ruined hinges and bolts on the door frame.

Presently one of them spoke and Carla translated, "There is no question but that the lock and hinges were deliberately damaged so the door would come off while the plane was in flight."

"How wicked!" Bess exclaimed.

Señor Ponte said they must get home as quickly as possible. He admitted feeling shaken himself. They drove off and it was not until they were halfway home that Nancy spoke.

"I'm sure it was my enemies who damaged the plane. They will go to any lengths to keep me from solving the mystery of the plaque."

"But, Nancy," Bess said, "how could they be sure that you would be standing by the door just when it came off?"

"They probably figured there was a chance the plane would be wrecked." Nancy shuddered. "When I think what could have happened to everyone, just because of me—!"

After a moment Señor Ponte patted her hand. "Do not chide yourself, my dear," he said. Nancy smiled at him.

When the girls reached the house, Señora Ponte had heard the story on a radio newscast and expressed her concern. "I immediately called the airport and was advised not to come there. All I could do was stay here and pray. You may be sure, my dears, I did plenty of that!"

Bess remarked, "This was the most exciting Sunday I've ever had," and the other girls agreed.

Nancy, Bess and George went to their rooms to rest until dinner-time. All of them fell asleep.

Later, as they were dressing, Bess remarked, "Nancy, I'm afraid you have not one or two enemies in this case, but many. We know of three. Two are in jail here in

South America and that awful Harry Wallace was arrested by the police in our country. Somebody else tampered with our plane."

George spoke up. "They aren't Nancy's private enemies," she said. "They're hostile to all of us."

The remark made Bess shudder, and Nancy advised, "Oh, let's not talk about this any more. If we don't change the subject we won't have any appetites for dinner." Nothing more was said and they went downstairs.

When Nancy learned that dinner was not ready, she asked Carla if she had any modelling clay.

"I'd like to try some of it on the plaque."

Carla was puzzled, but she went to get some. Nancy pressed lumps of it on to the surface of the plaque over the crossword cipher. In a few moments she took it out and looked to see if the imprint would reveal any clue.

"Girls, come here!" she called excitedly. "I think I've figured out something!"

Carla was the first to reach her friend's side. Nancy pointed out the imprint of the horizontal four-letter word at the base of the crossword cipher.

"I believe it's *mesa*. If I'm right, that only leaves the one word near the top that we haven't figured out."

Everyone wondered where the mesa might be which the Pontes' ancestor Aguilar had indicated.

"There are many tablelands in Peru," said Señor Ponte. "But one thing comes to my mind. Part of the story about the Indian who brought the plaque to my family was that he spoke Quechua. This might mean that the tableland referred to here could be the one at Machu Picchu."

"That is near Cuzco!" Carla said excitedly. "Father,

we were advised to go to Cuzco and talk to an old
Indian named Maponhni."

Bess spoke up. "Would the trip to Cuzco and Machu
Picchu cost very much?" she asked. "I'm running a
little low on funds."

Carla's father smiled. "I would like all of you girls
to be my guests on a sightseeing tour of those interesting
places. I have a feeling you will uncover some valuable
information and that would more than repay me for
the trip."

Nancy said at once, "Your offer is very generous,
Señor Ponte, but we shouldn't be such an expense to
you."

Señor Ponte grinned. "Do you know what the
Quechua Indians say to me? '*Canqui Japac.*'" His eyes
still twinkling, he translated. "It means, 'You are
rich.'"

Everyone laughed and George said, "I'm glad to
hear that. Since that is true, I accept your invitation,
Señor Ponte."

The other girls accepted too and it was decided that
they would go the day after tomorrow.

"It's going to be thrilling," Bess cried out.

"I cannot wait," said Carla. "I've never been to
those places before."

The following morning Señor Ponte suggested that
Carla show her friends more of the interesting sights in
Lima. "I think you would love the Torre Tagle Palace.
It is a rather elaborate Moorish style of architecture. The
place is now used by the Ministry of Foreign Affairs, so
only part of it is open to visitors."

Carla drove the girls to the ancient palace, now
hemmed in by business buildings. Before going inside,

her guests gazed at the elaborately carved wooden front of Torre Tagle. While they were admiring its lattice-windowed balcony on the first floor, Carla happened to glance across the street. A man stood there, his hat pulled low.

"He looks like Luis Llosa, that unpleasant assistant at Señor Velez's handicraft shop," she thought.

Quietly she alerted the other girls. As they turned to look, the man strolled away.

"I wonder what he was doing here," Nancy thought uneasily as she followed the others into the palace.

"How grand it must have been to live in such magnificence?" exclaimed Bess. They had paused in a central courtyard surrounded by a high balcony.

"Oh, look!" George exclaimed, pointing to a far corner where an ancient coach stood.

"My, how elegant!" said Nancy.

Red tieback curtains adorned the windows, and at the front, some distance ahead of the closed compartment, was the coachman's red-plush seat.

"I'll bet this was a four-horse coach," said George as she hurried over. "Boy, I would love to drive it!" She put her hand on the seat.

"I'd rather be a passenger, thank you," said Bess. She stepped forward in a stately manner. "I am Isabella, Queen of Spain. Hasten to the party, coachman, with my king and me."

Nancy laughed. "Wait a minute, Your Majesty. How about a photograph?"

Bess handed over her camera and said loftily, "I ought not to have my picture taken with a lowly coachman." Then, as she giggled and George snorted, Nancy snapped the shutter.

Carla had been watching in amusement. "Come," she said, leading the way up the stairs to the balcony. "I want to show you a special room."

They followed her along the balcony and through a room on to a shadowy porch. It was screened from view by the great wooden shutters they had admired from the street.

Carla explained that in olden times the women of the aristocracy rarely appeared on the streets, but they liked to watch the people below. "From here they could see without being seen."

Nancy walked to the window and peered through the shutters. She summoned the others and pointed across the street. There stood Luis Llosa!

"He has come back!" Carla whispered.

"To spy on us, I'll bet!" Bess added worriedly. The others agreed.

Carla shivered. "I hate to think that he was following us, but he must have been."

Bess said a bit fearfully, "When we leave here, he'll no doubt come after us!"

"So what? We can't stay here all day," George declared. "I'm going to scare him off!"

She opened one of the shutters and leaned out to look directly at Luis Llosa. He at once became ill at ease and quickly moved off.

'Let's go," Bess urged.

"All right," said Nancy. "But instead of going home, I'd like to stop at Señor Velez's shop and check on Llosa."

Carla drove directly there. When they walked into the shop, the owner greeted them affably. They told him about their trip to the arrayánes forest, their talk with the warden and their failure to find a single clue there.

"That's too bad," the craftsman remarked.

Nancy inquired if his assistant were there.

"No. I do not know why. He did not telephone. It is very strange. Perhaps he is ill."

Carla told him that the man was not ill and explained where the girls had seen him. Señor Velez said he could not understand it.

Nancy suspected that the man had taken the day off to shadow the girls. "But why?" she asked herself. "It has something to do with the plaque, I'm sure." She recalled his attempt to copy the carving, and was more convinced than ever that he had not acted out of simple curiosity.

Señor Velez spoke again. "Luis is a good worker, but he is a very strange and secretive person." The shop owner regarded the girls anxiously. "Why are you asking about him? Has he done something wrong?"

"Not that we know of," Nancy replied.

But in the minds of all the girls was the same grim question: *Had another dangerous enemy been revealed?*

11

The City of Gold

"LET's buy some gifts to take home," Bess suggested.

Nancy was brought out of her musing about Luis Llosa. She smiled. "That's a good idea."

The three girls from River Heights picked out various articles. Nancy purchased an attractive salad bowl set for her father and jewel cases for Hannah Gruen and Aunt Eloise.

After writing out the addresses where they were to be sent, she asked permission to go into the back room of the shop. It was here that the wooden objects were carved. When Nancy came to Luis Llosa's workbench, she paused. On it was a half-finished tray made of queñar wood.

As she glanced down to the floor, Nancy noticed another unfinished carving. She picked it up.

"I wonder what this was going to be," she murmured.

Señor Velez came into the room and she asked him about the object. He came over, took it and frowned.

"I do not know what this is intended for," he said.

The piece was about eight inches long and three-quarters of an inch thick, with a tube inside the centre of it.

"This is about the size and shape of handles of some

of our salad forks and spoons, but we always keep them solid," Señor Velez said.

"I found the wood under Luis Llosa's bench, so I suppose it's his," Nancy told him.

The shop owner frowned even more deeply. "No doubt, but this wood did not come from my purchases. It is arrayánes."

"What!" Nancy exclaimed.

"That is right," the craftsman told her. "I cannot understand. Luis must have brought it here. I intend to ask him when he returns." Señor Velez put the piece into his pocket.

Nancy's mind was already filled with speculations about Llosa's work. She said, "Maybe he intended to put something inside the handle."

"Perhaps," Señor Velez conceded. "But what? I will certainly make him tell me."

On the way home Nancy told the other girls of her discovery. Instantly George said, "I'm sure he's up to no good."

That evening Carla had arranged a delightful party for the North American girls to meet some of her Peruvian friends.

"It was wonderful and I enjoyed getting to know your friends," Nancy told Carla after the guests had left.

"And what marvellous dancers!" Bess exclaimed. "Oh, I could live here forever!"

"And have Dave down here fighting duels?" George grinned.

Before leaving for Cuzco the next day, Nancy telephoned Señor Velez. She found him upset. "My assistant has not come back and has sent no word. I called at his home to find out why, but nobody was there."

Nancy asked the shop owner if he had missed anything from his place of business. Señor Velez admitted that he had not thought of checking but would look immediately. "Hold the phone, please."

Within two minutes he was back. "Luis has taken many of my tools! Oh, it is dreadful, dreadful! Some of them are very old and I cannot replace them!"

"I am sorry," Nancy said. "You will report the theft to the police, of course?"

"Indeed, Indeed. And thank you, Miss Drew, for alerting me."

Bess, George and the Pontes were sorry to hear what had happened. They hoped that the police would pick up Luis Llosa quickly.

"I hope so too," said Nancy. "I am also interested in how Llosa got his arrayánes wood and what he was doing with it. Remember the police in Bariloche found a quantity of similar wood in Wagner's home. I feel sure he had been supplying Llosa with it."

"Of course," said George. "They're part of the same gang. The question is, what are they doing with this wood?"

Carla's mother said she was mortified that their old family mystery was causing such a fuss.

Her husband smiled. "My dear," he said, "aren't you pleased that these evil-doers are being apprehended?"

"Oh, yes," Señora Ponte replied. "But I wish the girls could have more fun and less worry."

Nancy put the plaque in her suitcase, then Carla's father drove the girls to the airport. The plane to

Cuzco was an old type which was not pressurized.

After it had been in the air a short while, the pilot announced that in order to go over the Andes they would have to fly at a great height, where the air was thin. The stewardess came to each passenger. She unfastened an oxygen tube from under the window and indicated that it was to be held near the mouth to keep from feeling faint.

The scenery below was very beautiful—mountain crags, forests and streams blended into a breathtaking panorama. About two and a half hours later the pilot announced that the oxygen tubes were no longer needed. The plane was coming down into Cuzco.

The girls from River Heights, seeing the city from the air, were amazed at its size. They had expected it to be much smaller.

"Imagine living in the mountains twelve thousand feet above sea level!" said Bess.

"Yes," George replied. "And I read in a guide-book this is known as a mountain-top valley. The people who lived here centuries ago were called 'valley people'. "

When the plane landed, the four girls found a taxi and Carla suggested that the driver take them for a quick tour round the city before going to the hotel.

Fortunately he spoke English and was evidently quite experienced in lecturing to tourists. He began by pointing out the huge stones in the old foundations of buildings. "They were built by the Incas. When the Spanish came, they tore down temples and palaces but left the foundations and put their own buildings on top of them."

The driver smiled. "The sun god punished them, though. When an earthquake came, the Spanish buildings fell over, but the foundations remained."

Next, he showed the girls a narrow Inca street. Both sides of it had high stone walls and the driver stopped so the visitors could walk down a short distance to see the famous twelve-sided stone which was part of it. Each girl counted the sides and marvelled at the way the ancient masons had trimmed this enormous rock to accommodate the ones fitted round it.

The young tourists noticed that all the stones fitted so perfectly that there was not one single opening or crack between them. Not even an earthquake could damage this amazing monument to ancient craftsmanship.

Presently the driver stopped again where a modern church had been built on the old Inca foundation. "This was where the Temple to the Sun once stood," he explained. "Beyond it, at that time, was a beautiful park with trees, flowers and golden statues. At the far end was a palace."

"How I wish," said Nancy, "that I could have seen them!"

The man smiled. "If you had been an Inca maiden, you would have been wearing a long, one-piece dress made of alpaca wool. Your hair would have been in long braids tied with many coloured ribbons of wool. You would have worn sandals, perhaps a sash, and a long shawl covering your head and hanging down the back."

"It sounds very attractive," she remarked.

"Perhaps you would like to buy such a dress for a souvenir," the guide suggested.

All the girls wanted Inca dresses, so he took them to a shop where they purchased colourful shifts, two

with zigzagging patterns in red and black, two with a
llama design woven into the cloth.

"I can't wait to wear mine at a party back home,"
Bess said, giggling.

When the shopping was complete, the driver took
the girls to their hotel and warned them to "take it
easy". "You would not want to get altitude sickness,"
he said, smiling. "Walk slowly while you are here."

They thanked him for the advice, but as soon as the
girls had had lunch, Nancy said she thought they
should find the old Indian Maponhni. She learned from
the desk clerk that the Indian was well known and he
directed the girls to the elderly man's home. It was on
a side street and proved to be of rather modern con-
struction.

Carla smiled. "I half expected that Maponhni
would be living in a stone hut with a thatched roof.
But the Indians who live here today are quite modern.
Many of them have transistor radios and are no longer
isolated from the rest of the world."

Nancy knocked on the door and it was opened
by a pleasant-looking man, definitely a descendant of
the Incas. He was of medium height, somewhat portly,
and had large hands with small wrists. His head was
broad, and he had high cheekbones and an aquiline
nose. The man's eyes were somewhat almond-shaped,
like an Oriental's, and his expression kindly and
humorous.

"Señor Maponhni?" Nancy asked.

The Indian grinned. "*Munanki! Imaynan caskianqui.*"
Nancy's eyes twinkled. "*Hucclla,*" she replied.
"*Yusul paiki.*"

Maponhni looked stunned. In English he said,

"You speak Quechua? Please come in, all of you."

Nancy laughed and told him that they had heard about him from the warden at the arrayánes forest and that he had taught them the words. "He said you know more about Inca history than anyone else."

"He flatters me," the Indian said. "But I will be happy to answer your questions."

Nancy, who was carrying the plaque, now unwrapped it. Carla told of the ancient mystery.

"We thought you might help us figure out the cross-word cipher."

Maponhni started to examine the monkey side of the plaque. Suddenly everyone noticed that all the objects in the room were shaking.

The Indian laid the plaque on a table. When it nearly fell off, Nancy grabbed the plaque. The old man had begun to chant in Quechua.

"What's happening?" Bess asked, looking around fearfully.

Carla's face was pale. "An earthquake!" she gasped.

· 12 ·

The Boy Spy

As the earth tremors continued, Maponhni stopped his chanting and motioned for the others to follow him. Quickly he led the way into the kitchen and said this was an original Inca building with a modern roof.

"We will be safe here, I think," he told them. "The old walls are sturdy."

From outside came the cries of people and the sound of objects falling. The girls followed the man's example of sitting cross-legged on the floor. No one spoke. All were too tense to do anything but wait. Then abruptly the shaking stopped.

Everyone heaved a sigh of relief and Carla said, "I hope this will not be followed by another quake."

Maponhni said quietly, "Who knows? But I think it is over."

Everyone was eager to go to the street and see what had happened.

"Be careful where you step," the Indian warned.

Just outside the front door a boy about fifteen years old was lying on the ground, swaying from side to side and mumbling.

"You're safe now," Nancy said to him kindly.

The boy's eyes were closed and he paid no attention to her. He kept on muttering the same thing over and over.

"What is he saying?" Bess asked the Indian.

Maponhni looked puzzled. "He is saying, 'Oh, Cat, I must stop. The sun god has sent this sign. You say the girl is a spy? . . . No, no. Go away, Cat. I will do nothing more for you.' "

"That's a lot of gibberish," George remarked. "What does he mean?"

"I do not know," Maponhni replied.

He shook the boy, who finally opened his eyes. He looked around dazedly as the Indian helped him to his feet, then questioned him in Quechua.

A sudden look of terror came into the youth's eyes. He stared hard at the four girls, gave a little cry as if in pain, and ran off down the street as fast as he could.

"Shall we chase him?" George asked.

"Yes!" cried Nancy.

Instantly Maponhni caught her arm. "No," he said. "The boy has done no harm and you should not run in this rare atmosphere."

"But he may be connected with our mystery," Carla stated. "He mentioned 'cat'—"

"We think this boy may be working for a man who calls himself El Gato," Nancy explained. "He is wanted by your police. He intends to harm us. The boy may report to him where we are and what we're doing!"

"I am sorry I stopped you," Maponhni said. "Now it is too late to find the boy."

Nancy asked the Indian if he had ever heard of a sinister character called El Gato.

"No. And I did not recognize the boy who mumbled those strange words. I know every Indian in Cuzco," he told the girls. "This boy is a stranger here."

"Then," said Carla, "he might have been sent to Cuzco by El Gato."

Nancy agreed, but said that perhaps the earthquake had frightened him so much he would not do any more work for El Gato. She explained to Maponhni about Carla receiving the anonymous note: *Beware of the cat.*

"That is not good," he said. "You girls take care."

The group went back to the house and once more the Indian looked at the plaque. He studied it for a long time, then finally confessed that he could make nothing out of either side.

"I can tell you something, though, which may help you," he said. "When I was a little boy I heard my great-grandmother tell a story which had been handed down in her family. It might concern your ancestor, Señorita Ponte.

"The story was about a fine Spanish artist-adventurer who came first to Cuzco and then went to Machu Picchu. He was well received by the people there and enjoyed his work. But after a while they made him a prisoner. We did not hear why.

"I do not know how long he was there," Maponhni continued, "but it seems that he and an Indian companion escaped. They made their way here.

"The Indian knew an Inca priest. He secretly befriended them. But when the priest tried to question the Spaniard about why he had been a prisoner, the artist refused to tell anything. Shortly afterwards, he and the Indian disappeared. Nothing more was ever heard of them. Years later, when the Inca priest was dying, he confessed to helping the runaways."

"Did the story tell what the Spaniard's name was?" Nancy asked. "Aguilar, perhaps?"

Maponhni shook his head. "The name I heard was not Spanish, but Quechuan. I have even forgotten what that was, but probably a name the Indians gave him."

"Why," Carla mused, "would the artist refuse to answer the Cuzco priest who befriended him?"

All the girls surmised that it might be because the man had discovered a secret he was afraid to tell. Or was he trying to keep some special information to himself until he could contact his family in Lima?

"Maybe," Carla said thoughtfully, "this man *was* Aguilar."

"It's quite possible," said Nancy. "After all, there were many adventurers at that time, but my guess is that a European artist in these parts was unusual."

Maponhni nodded. "You say you think this plaque indicates something valuable like a treasure? What do you expect to find—Inca gold?"

"Who knows?" George replied. "A really fabulous object may be buried somewhere. All we have to do is find the spot."

Maponhni advised them to spend a day or two at the ruins of Machu Picchu. "What destroyed the city is a great mystery. Probably you know that. Maybe your treasure is buried there."

The girls thanked the Indian for his help. Before they left, he asked if he might take them the next day to see the ruins at Sacsahuaman. "They are just outside of town and an amazing sight. Sacsahuaman was originally a fort."

The girls said they would like very much to go and would be ready at ten o'clock.

The following morning Maponhni came to their

hotel with his car and they started off. When they reached the ruins, the visitors stood in awe.

"How magnificent!" Nancy exclaimed, gazing at the high zigzagging stonework that formed the front of the fortress.

Maponhni said the wide three-tiered wall, made entirely of huge limestone boulders, was sixty feet high and eighteen hundred feet long.

"Some of these rocks weigh two hundred tons and were brought here without the aid of any kind of machinery. Men tumbled them end over end using strong, slender tree trunks for leverage."

"How did the workmen get one rock on top of the other?" Bess asked.

Maponhni said that great mounds of dirt were piled up and the stones rolled up them and put into place. "Then the mound would be made higher so the next rock could be raised to position."

"It's a fantastic piece of engineering," Nancy remarked. "I'd like to climb up and look around." The others decided to try it also.

"Go ahead, but be careful!" the Indian warned. "I will wait here."

While they had been talking, a car had driven on to the far side of the grassy area. It continued in a huge semicircle and stopped near the end of the fortress wall, about five hundred feet from the girls.

At first they thought there was only the driver, but suddenly a man rose from the rear seat and disappeared behind the last projection of the wall. He was carrying something half concealed under his jacket.

"What was he holding?" Carla asked.

"It looked like a big can," Nancy replied.

The girls hunted for tiny worn places in the rocks as footholds to pull themselves up towards the first level of the fortress. Nancy reached it ahead of the others and hurried along the pathway. Eager to get to the top, she climbed to the second tier and was soon out of sight of the others.

"What a place for a seige!" Nancy thought, gazing around, then she walked forward.

Near the end of the wall she started downward in a slanting direction. When she was about twenty feet from the ground she heard a noise above her. She looked up just in time to glimpse a man's leg disappearing round the adjoining bend in the zigzag wall.

Suddenly Nancy gasped in astonishment. On a large rock above her was the newly painted, crude face of a bright-red cat!

· 13 ·

El Gato

THE cat again!

"Maybe the man who painted it was El Gato himself, leaving his mark!" Nancy thought.

She tried to peer round the corner of the zigzag wall, but could not do so without losing her balance. "I wish I could see him!" she fumed.

Wondering if he might have returned to his car, Nancy turned to gaze below. The driver was still there, but the other man was not in sight.

Nancy changed her position to look upwards again. She saw an arm poke itself round the corner. The arm disappeared for a second, then re-appeared. This time the hand was holding a bucket with red paint dripping over the sides.

Nancy was puzzled. "Is the man going to add to his picture?" she thought.

As she stood fascinated by the prospect, the hand suddenly swung upwards. With great force the hidden figure threw the bucket of red paint directly towards her.

Nancy knew that she had to move in a hurry, but there was no place she could run from her precarious position! She must jump!

Hoping to land on the soft grass below, Nancy leaped

Nancy had no choice but to jump

off the side of the fortress. It was a long jump. She took it gracefully, but landed with bone-jarring impact and sat down, breathless, without moving. The can now lay in a red gooey mass not far from her.

"Oh!" she said aloud, hurting all over.

Moments later, Nancy heard a car engine start. Turning her head, she saw the back of a man as he stepped into the rear of the car. He crouched on the floor so that she could not see him. The car sped off along the far side of the fortress grounds and disappeared.

"Nancy!" The cry came from George, who was running at top speed towards her friend. "Whatever happened to you?"

Bess and Carla followed. All were anxious about Nancy. In a weak voice she assured them she would be all right in a few minutes. Then she told her story and pointed upwards.

"El Gato!" Carla exclaimed. "To think he followed us way out here! We are not safe any place!"

Bess said she was thankful the man had not harmed Nancy. "But I'm sure he meant to and there's no telling what he may try next."

Nancy agreed. "The cat picture is a warning, I think, and may have other significance."

As she remained where she was and watched, her three friends climbed up to look at the red cat face. They examined it closely but could find no clue to what it might mean—besides being a warning. Bess snapped a picture of it, saying that Nancy could study the photo and perhaps see something which they had missed.

Carefully they made their way down again. By this time Nancy felt better and all the girls walked back slowly to their car. Maponhni was shocked when he heard what had happened.

"If I had known that, I would have taken the man's licence number. But maybe I can help you another way. I will ask about this man at shops in Cuzco where paint is sold. Perhaps he bought the red paint there to make the cat on the rock."

The guide suggested that the trip to Machu Picchu be postponed until the next day.

Carla thought this was a good idea. But she insisted that they ask the clerks at the hotel not to tell anyone the girls were staying over. When they reached the hotel, Carla made her request and the men promised to keep the secret.

The girls went up in the elevator to their rooms. It had begun to rain and Bess said she was cold. There was a heater in the room and she not only turned it on, but also closed the windows.

George, meanwhile, had been reading a sign tacked to the door. It gave advice to tourists on what to do and what not to do in this high altitude.

"It says here," she told her cousin, "that one should rest with the window open and use the heating system as little as possible."

Bess sighed, turned off the heat, and opened the windows again. "I'll just have to freeze," she said.

George chuckled. "Here's something else for you, Bess. It says eat light meals!" As Bess made a face, her cousin went on, "And if you feel terrible, call room service and a waiter will give you oxygen."

About two hours later there was a knock on Nancy's door. She opened it to find Maponhni there.

He did not come in, but said, "I found the place in

town where the red paint was sold to a stranger. Would this description fit anybody you know: dark hair, small, shifty eyes, and very hairy arms?"

Together Nancy and Carla cried out, "Luis Llosa!"

"Where is he from?"

"Lima," Nancy replied. "We suspect he may be the man who calls himself El Gato."

Bess and George had come into the hall, and Bess asked, "But how in the world could Luis Llosa have traced us here, or have learned we were going to the fortress?"

George answered the question. "A slippery character like that probably has a way of finding out everything he wants to know about people he's trailing. It wouldn't surprise me if Llosa shows up at Machu Picchu."

"Then I'm not going there," Bess said with determination. "He might try to harm us!"

Maponhni smiled. "My dear Miss Marvin," he said, "you must not miss Machu Picchu. It is one of the great ruins of the world. I will alert the police here to be on the look-out for this man to see that he does not take the train to Machu Picchu and I will go with you."

Bess looked relieved. "Good, and I hope they catch him! All right, I'll go." She chuckled. "If Luis Llosa is in Cuzco, maybe I'd be safer at Machu Picchu."

The next morning the girls set off with Maponhni. Nancy carried the plaque in her suitcase.

The tourists were intrigued by the one-car train which was more like an oversized tram-car. It climbed steadily up from the city, then suddenly stopped and went backwards.

"I wonder what is wrong," said Carla.

A passenger across the aisle from her explained, "Nothing is wrong. This railroad has a couple of switchbacks." When Carla looked puzzled, the man added, "It would be impossible for this train to climb straight up the mountain, so at certain points it runs backwards on a switch for a short distance. Then it goes forward again up the grade on still another track. By doing this a few times, the engineer can reach great heights quickly and without strain on the machinery."

"I see," Carla replied, although she was not sure she understood.

During the two-hour trip the train wound in and out among the mountains, many of them snow-capped, with corn growing at their base, where it was warm. Farther on, the train followed a valley and crossed several bridges over the winding Urubamba River.

The engineer made a few stops at stations. There were thatched Indian cottages nearby. Bright-eyed children crowded round the visitors and gladly accepted packets of sweets which the girls had brought along.

"They're adorable children," said Bess, "and they look happy, but certainly poor."

"Yes," Nancy agreed. "Don't you long to do something for them?"

Finally the train reached the little station at Machu Picchu. Buses were waiting to take the travellers up the mountainside to the hotel which stood near the ruins. On the way the sky suddenly clouded over and in moments rain began to fall.

"Oh dear!" Bess complained. "We've come all this way and now we won't be able to see anything!"

Maponhni smiled knowingly. "Here in the mountains there is much mist, but usually it does not last long.

Sometimes it turns to rain and then like magic the sun is suddenly out again. Do not worry. We shall see the ruins."

When they reached the hotel, Nancy was so fascinated by the scenery that she did not want to go inside. Far below, the Urubamba River looked like a snaking piece of brown ribbon. Above were mountain peaks and here and there she glimpsed the terraced flower and vegetable gardens used by the ancient Incas.

"Don't stand there in the rain," George said to her. "You'll get soaked. Let's register."

Nancy went inside with the others and they were assigned rooms. The desk clerk told them that lunch would be served in a short time. Since there were so many visitors, it would be necessary to have two sittings. "Miss Drew, will your group please come to the first one?"

"You bet I will," Bess spoke up, laughing. "I'm starved."

George gave her cousin a withering look. "Don't forget the instructions on the hotel door in Cuzco. 'Eat light.' "

Bess always made a little face at George in return for such a reprimand. "I have to keep up my strength to climb," Bess defended herself.

The girls hurried upstairs to unpack and Nancy put the plaque in a drawer. Then they met Maponhni in the dining room at a table near a long, open window. George sat with her back to it.

The Indian's bright eyes watched the girls intently as the first course was served. It was a typical native dish—a massive corn on the cob served with a large slice of Swiss cheese.

As Bess looked at her portion, she asked, "Maponhni, do we put this cheese on the corn or eat it separately?"

"Eat it any way you like," he replied.

Bess broke off a piece of the cheese and laid it on the kernels. She was about to take a bite when she glanced through the window. Her eyes grew large.

"George!" Bess cried. "Look out! That beast behind you is going to bite!"

· 14 ·

Alpaca Antics

As George jumped up and dashed away from the open window, Maponhni began to laugh.

"Your 'beast' is really very friendly," he said. "It is an alpaca—a grass-eating animal—and gentle."

To prove this he stepped to the next table where part of a plate of salad had been left. The Indian picked up a lettuce leaf and held it out to the alpaca. The animal nibbled it quickly.

George took another piece and extended it to the alpaca. She chuckled. "I'm sorry, old boy, but we don't happen to serve grass in this dining room."

The remark made Bess giggle. Getting up her courage, she too offered a piece of lettuce to the animal. When the girls stopped feeding him, their reproof was an indignant *na-aah, na-aah!*

At that moment a waiter came in with a tray of food. He set it down, went to the window, and clapped his hands. In Spanish he told the beast to go away. Lazily the alpaca walked off, its sheep-like head held disdainfully above its long neck.

"Oh girls! His family!" Carla exclaimed.

On the roadway just below the hotel stood a female and two baby alpacas.

"Aren't they darling?" said Bess. "I must take some pictures of them later."

Maponhni told the girls that alpaca fleece was valuable. "Generally it is white, but sometimes has grey or brown hair mixed in. The wool is soft enough to be used for clothing, and is very expensive."

"Is that the finest wool there is?" George queried.

The Indian shook his head. "The wool from the vicuña is the finest in the world. The animal looks very much like the alpaca, but is a little smaller. Its fleece is soft and silky.

"In Inca times only royalty and aristocracy were allowed to use this wool. It is said that the Inca himself, ruler of the whole nation, had the finest kind of garments, most of them made from vicuña wool. But after the first wearing, they were destroyed."

"What a dreadful waste!" George exclaimed.

"I agree," said Maponhni. "Furthermore, those precious things were lost for all time. Had they been saved, we could have enjoyed looking at them."

The Indian mentioned that a third animal in Peru whose fleece was used was the llama. "He's larger than the other two."

Maponhni said that the llama had been a beast of burden in Peru for many, many centuries. "Its wool is coarse and greasy, and is used mostly for heavy blankets, sacks, rope and halters for beasts. Of course, cloth for the very poor people has been woven from it since ancient times."

"They probably used the hides to make sandals," Carla suggested.

"I'll bet," George said with a grin, "that those old Incas wore the soft leather next to their skin so they wouldn't itch from the prickly wool!"

The others laughed. By the time they had finished

lunch, the rain had ceased and Bess urged the group to go outside so she could take some snapshots of the alpacas. After taking a couple of pictures, Bess handed the camera to Nancy.

"Please snap a picture of me seated on the alpaca," she said. "And don't let anybody slap him so he'll run away!"

Nancy took the camera and Bess walked forward. She swung herself up on to the back of the animal. "Ready!" she called out.

Instantly the alpaca bent its knees and sat down in the roadway.

"Oh, you mean old thing!" Bess scolded. She slapped the animal gently. "Stand up!"

When the alpaca did not obey, Nancy laughingly snapped the picture, anyway.

Maponhni walked forward and with a chuckle said, "Miss Marvin, you must weigh more than a hundred pounds. That is the limit of a burden an alpaca will carry. He cannot be coaxed. You may as well get off."

She grinned, but did not reveal her weight. She got off the animal and instantly changed the subject.

"I'm ready now to take pictures of the ruins."

Nancy herself was eager not only to see the great archaeological wonder, but to hunt for a clue to the mystery of the crossword cipher. From the hotel, Maponhni led the way up a path to an admission stand where they paid a small fee. Then they began the climb.

To their left the mountainside rose steeply and was an amazing sight of endless series of three- to five-foot stone-faced terraces. They varied from fifteen to thirty feet in width.

Running up alongside the terraces were many stone staircases. From them branched alleyways between stone huts in various states of ruin. Maponhni explained that originally the dwellings stood from eight to ten feet in height and had thatched roofs.

"Archaeologists believe that the workers lived on one side of the city, the aristocracy on the other. They think this because one section was better built and had larger rooms than the other. At the very top stood a fine building that was like a convent. The Chosen Virgins of the Sun lived there. These maidens spent their entire time in religious work, like the nuns today, and did a lot of weaving."

Bess looked to her right, where the ground fell steeply to the river. "It would be easy to tumble down out of this city and drop all the way to the water," she said with a shudder.

"Don't look down," George advised.

The girls followed their guide as he wound in and out of the narrow, ancient streets. Nancy tried to imagine what the place had looked like when it was a flourishing city.

She entered one building which was larger than any of the others she had seen. It had several connecting rooms and Nancy concluded that this might have been the home of a high official.

By the time she returned to the entrance, her companions were out of sight. Thinking they had gone down the steep flight of steps nearby, she went after them. When Nancy reached the foot, the others were not around, so she walked forward to the edge of the path and gazed down the precipitous drop at the jungle-like valley.

As she contemplated the gorgeous view with mountains in the distance, Nancy became aware of a thudding sound behind her. Turning, she was horrified to see a huge bundle of thatch rolling at fast speed in her direction. Should it hit her, she would be swept off the mountainside. Just before it reached her, Nancy gave a mighty leap and hurdled the bundle.

"Oh!" she cried out as the thatch tumbled over the edge and disappeared.

As she stood trembling, Nancy heard a man's voice and looked off to one side to see who he was. An Indian workman was busy putting thatch on a roof of one of the stone huts which was being restored. He pointed up the steps.

"Señor!" he called out.

Nancy looked there but could see nothing. She wondered whether the bundle had been accidentally dislodged by someone, or thrown on purpose.

The workman kept on pointing excitedly and calling, "Señor!"

Nancy was convinced now that he had seen someone throw the bundle. Running up to him, she asked, "Who was it? What did he look like?"

The workman raised his hands in a helpless gesture to indicate he did not speak English.

"*Español?*" Nancy asked, thinking she might manage a few simple phrases in Spanish.

Again the man shook his head. She assumed he spoke Quechua. She would find Maponhni and bring him back to question the workman. "Maybe he can get a clue to the señor this man's talking about."

Nancy had a long hunt before she was able to locate the others. Immediately Bess hugged her friend.

"Nancy! We've been looking for you because we wanted to go after that dreadful Luis Llosa!"

"What do you mean?"

"We saw him among the ruins!" said Carla.

Upon hearing of Nancy's adventure, the others were sure that Llosa had tossed the bundle of thatch in her direction.

"If he's here, we'll find him!" George vowed. "Come on! Let's separate and track him down!"

· 15 ·

Telltale File

BESS and George and Carla hurried off.

Before Nancy began her search she turned to Maponhni. "Will you go back and talk to that workman? I think he speaks Quechua. Find out what the señor he mentioned looked like."

"I will do that. Then I will start a search too for this Luis Llosa," the Indian promised.

By this time several groups of tourists had arrived to see the ruins. As each girl came upon a group, she asked if anyone had seen a man who answered the description of Llosa. None of them had.

On one of the staircases Bess encountered a young man. He stopped climbing, but instead of answering her question, he motioned for her to sit on the steps with him.

"Thank you. I will stand," Bess replied.

In broken English the stranger told her he was a Peruvian. "You are beautiful girl from North America," he said. "I like you. We make date maybe?"

In her own mind Bess decided that he was the last person in the world with whom she wanted to make a date. She did not answer but repeated her question. "Have you seen a man who is thin and dark and has shifty eyes?"

The young man began to laugh. "You forget about that one. Tonight we make date?"

Bess was furious. She turned away and began to climb the steps. The Peruvian laughed. "Oh, you afraid of me? You are American girl they say is choosy?"

"I certainly am," Bess said with dignity, and hurried up the steps with the speed of a frightened alpaca. Her admirer did not try to follow. By the time Bess reached the top step, she was winded and had to sit down.

"George was right. I shouldn't have eaten all that corn and Swiss cheese," she berated herself. Then she thought wistfully, "Why couldn't he have been one of the nice young Peruvian men—like the ones Carla introduced us to!"

Bess remained quiet, even after she had stopped gasping. She could vaguely hear two men talking somewhere near her. The men were coming closer. In a few moments what they were saying became very distinct. At first Bess paid no attention, thinking they were tourists talking about a group of girls.

But suddenly she was shocked when one man, who sounded like Luis Llosa, said, "You tell Nancy Drew she is a nuisance in Peru. She must go home at once!"

Bess's heart began to pound. There was no question in her mind but that the voice belonged to Luis Llosa. What should she do? Should she let the man know she had heard him and demand an explanation?

"But he might harm me," was her second thought, "and then I couldn't warn Nancy."

Nevertheless, Bess decided to be courageous. She got up and looked around for the two speakers, but could see no one. Bess ran up and down a few of the ancient alleyways but could not find Luis Llosa.

"I must alert Nancy!" she thought.

Trying to find her proved to be hopeless. Bess called Nancy's name several times but received no answer.

Presently another thought came to Bess. Suppose Luis Llosa was on his way to the hotel to steal the precious plaque! Probably he knew that Nancy had retrieved it from the gift shop. Bess figured that the gang had not been able to decipher any more than the girls had.

"I'll bet they don't want Nancy to keep the plaque for fear she'll solve its mystery before they can. I'd better hurry back and stop Llosa from getting it!"

Bess ran practically all the way to the hotel. She obtained the key to Nancy and Carla's room, quickly ran up the stairs, and let herself in. Then she locked the door and immediately dashed to the drawer where the plaque had been placed. It was still there!

"Thank goodness!" Bess exclaimed.

She sat down in a chair to catch her breath and wait. Minutes passed. No one came. Bess was beginning to think that her hunch had been wrong, when she heard footsteps in the hall. They stopped in front of the door.

Bess held her breath and listened. No key was inserted into the lock, but the doorknob turned. Then she heard a scraping sound.

"Someone is trying to force the door open!" she thought. "Oh, what shall I do?" She was afraid to keep still but more afraid to cry out.

Tensely Bess watched the door. Presently a long, thin file came sliding through the crack. Within moments the implement protruded into the room about two inches.

Bess's mouth was dry with fright. "In another moment that intruder will get in!" she thought wildly. "And no telephone here!"

A sudden idea came to her. She crossed the room softly, grabbed the file, and gave it a hard yank. The whole tool came through the crack!

Instantly she heard angry mutterings in the hall. Someone kicked the door, then ran down the hall. Bess was so amazed and relieved that she flopped onto the bed, still clutching the file.

In the meantime, the other girls and Maponhni had continued to hunt through the ruins and question people about the mysterious señor. Finally George encountered a broad-shouldered woman with a deep, husky voice.

In response to the girl's query, she looked hard at her questioner. "I don't know what girls are coming to these days. Always chasing a man. Is this one you're after somebody who wants to get away from you?"

"Oh no," George said quickly. "It's nothing like that—"

The woman interrupted her. "That's what all girls say, but I know better. You're after him and you're determined to find him."

George smiled. "You're right, but my interest in finding him is because he's a thief!"

The woman's eyes bulged. "A thief! Well, why didn't you say so in the first place?"

George felt like telling her she had had no opportunity, but repeated her original question. "Please tell me if you saw him."

"Yes, I did," the woman replied.

"The Lima police are looking for him," George told her.

The woman pointed in the direction of the girls' hotel. "The man was heading down there," she said. "If you want to catch him, you'd better hurry."

George thanked her, and as the young sleuth hastened away, the woman called, "I'm sorry I said what I did to you." George waved at her and smiled.

Upon reaching the hotel, George got the key to her room and went upstairs. As she unlocked the door, Bess opened the one to Nancy's room.

"Oh, George, I'm so glad to see you. Something dreadful happened." She held up the file and poured out her story.

Her cousin was amazed. "You sure came through that time," George said. "By the way, I hurried back here because a woman up at the ruins told me Luis Llosa was headed this way. Probably he was the person with the file."

"I'm sure he was," Bess replied. "And thank goodness he has left here."

"What do you mean?" George asked.

Bess explained that she had looked out of the window and had seen Luis Llosa drive off a short time before in a private car.

"This was the only reason I dared unlock the door and come into the hall just now."

Bess went on to tell the bits of conversation she had overheard in the ruins. "I wonder who the man was that Luis Llosa was talking to. He may still be around and harm Nancy!"

"You're right," George agreed. "We must warn her."

She took the file from Bess and walked to the window in Nancy's room to examine the tool carefully.

"I suppose Llosa's fingerprints are on it," she said, "but ours are also." An instant later she said excitedly, "Look! There's a name on here—Velez. I'll bet this file was stolen from Jorge Velez's shop!"

Both girls were sure that it was one of the tools Luis Llosa had stolen from his employer's workroom.

George tossed the file on the dressing-table. "Let's go!" she urged. "We must find Nancy."

Suddenly the sunlight outside faded and it began to rain hard.

At the same moment Carla came into the room. "I just made it," she said. "Maponhni is downstairs. He said we were going to have a downpour. By the way, the description that workman in the ruins gave him of the señor matches Luis Llosa perfectly."

"That villain!" George cried out indignantly. "And listen to this!"

She and Bess told the story of the threat to Nancy and showed Carla the file.

Carla was amazed. "By the way, where is Nancy?" she inquired.

George suggested that since all the tourists were coming back because of the rain, Nancy might be downstairs talking with some of them. The girls locked their doors and went to the ground floor.

People were milling about the lobby and the lounge of the hotel. Nancy was not among them. The girls found Maponhni seated on a chair in a corner of the lounge. When he heard that Nancy had not returned and was told the other events of the afternoon, he became alarmed.

"This man Luis Llosa—after he drove off, he could have sneaked back on foot and found Miss Drew in the ruins!"

"Yes," Carla agreed. "And do not forget the man he was talking to. Oh dear, why did I ever get Nancy into this dreadful mess!"

"There is only one thing for us to do," George said grimly. "We must all go back and find Nancy at once, rain or no rain!"

· 16 ·

Sacred Stones

THE worried searchers, wearing raincoats and hats, hurried up the roadway that led to the ruins. As soon as they reached the mass of devastated buildings, all of them began calling loudly:

"Nancy! Nancy!"

The only sounds were the echoes of their own voices.

Bess was on the verge of tears. "Oh, I just know something dreadful has happened to Nancy!"

George looked at her sternly. "Nancy has a knack of getting out of tight spots. Let's keep our thoughts optimistic."

"You're right, George," Bess admitted, and tried to look less gloomy.

Maponhni and the girls went on, calling out every few minutes. There was still no response from Nancy.

Carla was very quiet but the others could see she was alarmed. Finally she said, "Maybe Nancy was a prisoner in Luis Llosa's car when he drove away. Perhaps we should go back and report her disappearance to the police."

For the first time Maponhni spoke up. "When we were up here before, we did not go down the other side of this peak. I suggest we look there before we give up."

The others followed him up the steep incline to the

top, then looked down the far side of the mountain.

"There she is!" Bess shouted with joy. "And she's all right!"

Down the grassy, bush-strewn slope was a picturesque sight. Four poles had been erected and a poncho stretched across the top of them. On the ground underneath the shelter sat Nancy and an elderly Indian. She was busy writing, apparently taking down what the old man was saying. She seemed to be unaware of her friends at the summit.

As quickly as they could, Maponhni and the girls made their way down the wet, slippery mountainside.

George called out in a loud voice, "Nancy!"

This time she looked up. "Oh, I'm getting some wonderful clues!" Nancy called back. "Maponhni, I'm so glad you came. This man speaks only Quechua. I've been trying to write down the way the words sound."

When the others reached her, Nancy introduced her companion. His name was Pansitimba. The newcomers acknowledged the introduction and gave their own names.

Then Bess said to Nancy, "If this man doesn't speak English or Spanish, how in the world did you get him to talk?"

Nancy grinned. "I said to him, '*Munanki! Imaynan caskianqui?*' Remember? 'Hello! How are you?' "

The others smiled, and Carla asked, "Then what did you do?"

"I said to him, 'Did you ever hear of a man named Aguilar?' "

She related that upon hearing the name he had looked at her strangely and had begun to talk very fast.

"He kept repeating Aguilar so often, I finally decided to try writing down all the words as best I could and ask Maponhni to translate them."

Pansitimba had said nothing to the newcomers, but upon hearing the name Aguilar again, he began to talk to Maponhni. One of the first things he said was:

"*Warm ccate cachaussua.*"

"Wow! That's a mouthful!" George remarked. "What does it mean?"

Maponhni was grinning broadly. "It means," he said, then paused. "It means, 'Is that girl a spy?'"

"Oh goodness!" exclaimed Carla, and the other girls laughed.

Their guide quickly explained the girls' mission to the elderly Indian and he too smiled. For several minutes after that the two men talked. Pansitimba made various gestures with his arms and pointed to the ruins, with Maponhni nodding understandingly. Finally he translated the conversation to the girls.

"There is a legend in Pansitimba's tribe that an ancestor of his had been a special servant to a Spaniard named Aguilar. Somehow he had learned about Machu Picchu and came here to see it."

Maponhni went on to say that these ancient Indians, who had never seen a white man, had thought Aguilar a god. This was partly because he was white, but mostly because he was a very good artist. He had brought paper, paints and brushes with him and made fine portraits of the Inca ruler and the city officials.

"But after a while they became afraid of Aguilar because he knew so much and the priests thought he might gain control of the people, so they made him a prisoner."

"How sad!" Bess put in.

Maponhni smiled. "Aguilar was very clever and did not remain a prisoner long. He got out and fled from this place. Pansitimba's ancestor, the servant, went with him. No one ever saw either of them again."

"What a fascinating story!" said Nancy.

Carla nodded. "Now we know that the artist Maponhni told us about really was Aguilar."

Nancy agreed and said, "Maponhni, will you ask Pansitimba if the story mentions a treasure in connection with the Spaniard or his servant?"

The question was put and the reply translated. The man had heard of none.

"Ask him also," said Nancy, "if there is a legend in his tribe about what happened to Machu Picchu."

Before the old Indian could answer, there was a sudden terrific downpour and with it a strong gust of wind. The poles and poncho went sailing through the air. Pansitimba groaned. He was no longer agile enough to run after them.

"I'll get it!" cried George, realizing how precious the man's shelter was to him, and took off after the poncho.

The tent poles had fallen to the ground and were rolling down the steep mountainside. The other girls dashed after the poles.

The poncho was being tossed in circles, making it difficult for George to grab it. Fortunately, a sudden down draught brought the garment near her. Stretching up her arms, she caught hold of one end and held on tightly.

In the meantime, the other girls were scrambling hither and thither to rescue the poles. Nancy grabbed two and each of the others retrieved one.

As Carla glanced at Nancy again, she said, "You are soaked! We must go right back to the hotel so that you can change your clothes." She smiled mischievously. "You have a habit of getting all wet on my account."

Nancy grinned and said if one of the girls would just lend her a dry sweater she would be all right. "I want to hear the rest of Pansitimba's story," she said.

"It may be a long one," Bess warned her. "Why don't we invite Pansitimba to the hotel? It wouldn't hurt him to do a little drying out too."

When the invitation was extended to the old man, he smiled appreciatively but declined. Nancy asked Maponhni to tell him the girls very much wanted him to come.

"I would like to show him the plaque. Maybe he can figure out something we have been unable to decipher."

After the guide had translated the message, Pansitimba accepted. The group walked slowly to the hotel. Nancy immediately went upstairs, changed her clothes, and dried her hair. Before coming down again, the young detective wrapped the plaque in a sweater and brought it along.

By the time she reached the lounge, Pansitimba's hair and clothing seemed to be dry and she urged him to go on with his story.

"You are interested in knowing why Machu Picchu became a ruin?' Maponhni asked, and all the girls nodded.

After a lengthy conversation between the two Indians, Maponhni said, "There is another legend in Pansitimba's tribe. Not long after Aguilar had fled from Machu Picchu, a band of Spanish explorers and some

Indians who had been converted to Spanish ways came and sacked the city. There was a dreadful time. They carried off the maidens and nearly all the women, but they killed most of the men and threw their bodies into the river."

"How utterly ghastly!" Bess murmured.

Maponhni went on, "Nothing was left, so there are no pictures or carvings or artefacts to show what this glorious city once looked like."

Nancy spoke up. "One thing I cannot understand is what happened to all the rest of the large stones which the Indians must have used in building their houses and temple."

Maponhni put the question to Pansitimba. The elderly Indian shrugged and replied, "It is said that afterwards people came here and took the stones away. Since this was supposed to be a sacred city and a refuge, they no doubt thought having one of the stones in their home would bring them good fortune."

When Pansitimba finished, Nancy unwrapped the plaque and had Maponhni tell him about it.

"Please ask him," Nancy requested, "if he can supply the missing letters."

Pansitimba studied them a few minutes. Then Maponhni asked Nancy for a sheet of paper and a pencil. She took them from her purse. Slowly and painstakingly, Pansitimba began to copy the letters from the plaque on to the paper. When he had written *mono cola* and *mesa*, the girls held their breath.

Was the mystery word near the top of the crossword cipher going to be deciphered at last?

· 17 ·

A Smuggler

"THE final word," Carla cried out, "is *china!*"

"What does it mean?" Nancy asked quickly.

Carla said that in Spanish it stood for many things—Chinese, china, porcelain. "It even means pebbles."

"Pebbles!" Nancy repeated. She looked off into the distance and then said, "Perhaps we should look for a *mesa* of pebbles."

"With a monkey's tail on it!" George added, grinning.

The others laughed, then there was a prolonged silence as the girls tried to figure out in which sense Aguilar had used *china*. Did the *mesa* have Chinese living on it, or was it perhaps a spot where porcelain was made?

Suddenly the old Indian said something to Maponhni. The guide in turn became excited and the two men talked at a rapid rate.

The girls looked at one another, puzzled, but presently Maponhni turned to them and said, "I think Pansitimba has solved your mystery for you. Have you ever heard of the Nascan lines?"

Carla spoke up. "I have heard of them, but I really don't know anything about the place."

Maponhni explained. "About two hundred miles

south of Lima there is a desert—a pebbly *mesa* twelve hundred feet above sea level and fifty miles from the ocean.

"In ancient times—and no one knows how long ago—people there scratched giant figures into the earth. These designs can still be seen and are named for the Nascan people whose pottery was found nearby. I have never been to the Nascan site, but I have been told that from a plane you can see everything. There are lines like on your plaque and figures of many things, including monkeys."

Nancy was so excited she felt as if her heart had suddenly stopped beating. "That's it!" she exclaimed. "Oh, this is simply marvellous! How can we ever thank Pansitimba for giving us this clue?"

Maponhni translated the message to Pansitimba, who merely smiled and shook his head. He wanted them to know he was a very religious and philosophical man who never took earthly rewards for helping people.

Bess's eyes suddenly became dewy and she murmured, "It is a privilege to meet such a person."

When this was translated to Pansitimba, he looked embarrassed and turned to leave.

"Wait!" said Nancy, and invited Pansitimba to eat with them.

He shook his head and Maponhni smilingly said that the old Indian was too shy to go into the dining room. He was not used to eating in this fashion and also he did not like the kind of food they served.

"I'm sorry," Nancy said. "Before he goes, I would like to know something. Pansitimba seems to have remarkable eyesight. Even at his age he was able to read things on the plaque which we could not see through a magnifying glass."

"I can answer that," Maponhni replied. "Many Inca Indians in these mountains have inherited amazing sight. Pansitimba can see tiny things at close range and spot small objects and read signs two-thirds of a mile away."

The girls were astounded to hear this and George said, "I'd like a demonstration."

They walked outside with Pansitimba, and Maponhni said something to him in Quechua. At once Pansitimba looked far off. Then he spoke to Maponhni, who translated:

"Our friend sees a condor seated on top of a tree. I cannot see it. Can you?" He pointed down towards the river.

All the girls confessed they could not see anything but dense growth. A few moments later Pansitimba proved to be right. A huge condor rose into the air and winged its way up the mountainside.

"That's fantastic!" Bess burst out. "Oh, what I wouldn't give to have sight like that!"

Maponhni translated and Pansitimba smiled. Then he turned once more to leave.

Nancy called out, *"Cutimunaikicama."*

Pansitimba turned round and gave her a big smile for saying goodbye to him in his language, and repeated the phrase.

The girls were ready early the next morning to leave Machu Picchu. During the ride back to Lima, first by train to Cuzco, then by plane, they felt it best not to talk about the mystery in public. Each girl kept a sharp look-out for Luis Llosa but did not see him.

"Are you going to call the police as soon as we get to the Ponte home?" George asked Nancy.

She shook her head. "The first thing I want to do is go to Señor Jorge Velez's shop with the file. We must find out definitely if it belongs to him and also whether he has heard from his assistant."

As soon as the plane landed in Lima, the girls said goodbye to Maponhni and paid him for his excellent services. He had travelled all the way with them to do some shopping in the city.

Carla hailed a taxi and gave the address of the craft shop. Señor Velez expressed delight at seeing the girls again, but his face clouded when they told him of their adventures and suspicions. He identified the file at once and said Luis Llosa had not reported for work, nor had he ever communicated with the shop.

"Señor Velez," said Nancy, "you have already told us that nothing seemed to be missing except tools, but have you looked in your work-benches and desks to see if any other articles are missing?"

The shop owner admitted he had not. He headed first for the spot where Luis Llosa had worked. The girls followed him to the back room and watched as he pulled open first one drawer, then another of the table that stood against an inner wall.

A strange look came over Señor Velez's face. "Every drawing of mine he was using is gone," he reported. "Apparently Luis took them all."

Nancy's sharp eyes had detected an unusual back panel in one of the drawers. She asked the shop owner if he would mind if she investigated it.

"No indeed. Go ahead."

Nancy pulled the drawer all the way out and set it on top of the work-bench. It was quite evident that the space in this drawer was less than in that of similar ones. At the back a large section of wood had been nailed in as if to reinforce the drawer.

Suspicious, Nancy asked Señor Velez for the file which they had brought. When he handed it to her, she wedged the file alongside the extra piece of wood and pried it forward. A moment later the section, which was hollow, pulled free. Underneath lay several letters.

Nancy picked up one of the envelopes and saw that it was addressed to Luis Llosa, evidently at his home in Lima.

"Look!" she exclaimed, pointing to the sender's name and address in the upper left-hand corner.

"Harry Wallace!" Carla cried out. "The importer who tried to take the plaque from your home, Nancy!"

As George told the story to the shop owner, Nancy pulled out one of the letters and unfolded it. The others crowded round her to read it, and expressed astonishment at the contents.

The salutation was "Dear El Gato" and the letter stated that the shipment had arrived all right and a cheque was enclosed. The note ended with praise for El Gato's cleverness in handling the order.

Nancy turned to Señor Velez. "Did you know Luis Llosa's nickname was El Gato?"

"I certainly did not," the man replied.

"He's on the police 'wanted' list," Nancy said.

"I shall call headquarters at once," declared Señor Velez.

While he went off to do this, Nancy examined every drawer in Luis Llosa's workbench for additional secret compartments.

"Maybe we can find out what he was shipping."

The other girls helped her pull out the drawers and set them on top of the work-bench. Each was examined thoroughly. Nancy noticed that the bottom of one was thicker than that of the others.

"Maybe this means something," she said.

Again using the file, she managed to pry up part of the wooden bottom and found that there was another beneath it. Between the two pieces of wood lay a matching salad fork and spoon.

"They are made of arrayánes wood!" Bess remarked.

"And I'll bet the handles are hollow," George added.

Nancy was already experimenting to see if she could unscrew one of the handles. She did so with little effort. Peering inside, the girls could see a quantity of fine white power.

Just then two police officers arrived and Señor Velez led them into the workroom. He introduced the girls and explained their part in solving the mystery.

Nancy held up the spoon handle and showed it to the officers. "I believe El Gato is a smuggler," she said.

One of the officers took the wooden implement and smelled the contents. "I am not sure what this is," he said. "I will take it to the police laboratory for analysis."

He had barely finished speaking when George happened to glance towards an open window. She saw a head rising up over the sill. Then she recognized the face of Luis Llosa!

Before George could cry out, his hand came up and he hurled a bomb with a lighted fuse into the workroom.

"On the floor, everybody!" George screamed.

Instantly the whole group dived and lay still. The

bomb hit Llosa's work-bench and exploded. Bits of shattered wood, pots of varnish, and cans of paint flew in all directions. Everyone in the room was pelted with debris.

As soon as things quietened down, Nancy and the others cautiously got to their feet. Velez, excited, began to speak half in Spanish and half in English.

George pointed to the window and said, "Luis Llosa threw the bomb."

The two officers dashed from the room and the others heard the shop door slam.

"Did anyone get hurt?" Nancy asked.

Fortunately, the home-made bomb had not been a powerful one and its victims in the workroom had suffered only minor cuts and bruises.

Bess, however, was on the verge of hysterics. "Nancy, that bomb was aimed right in your direction! If you hadn't ducked, it would have hit you. Oh, Nancy, you might have been killed!"

Nancy was pretty subdued herself. She doubted that the bomb could have killed her, but Luis Llosa certainly intended that it do a good bit of damage. She decided that he had hoped to destroy all the evidence against him.

"Llosa must have followed us from the airport and had the bomb with him."

"Oh, I hope the police catch him!" Carla said nervously. "None of us is safe while he is at large."

She told Señor Velez the whole story of the cat warning she had received and the red cat face painted on the rock at Sacsahuaman.

"It is a dreadful business," the craftsman said. He picked up the spoon handle which the officer had laid down. "I wonder what this white powder can be."

He sprinkled a small quantity into the palm of his hand, raised it to his mouth, and stuck out his tongue to test it.

"Oh, please don't do that!" Nancy advised hurriedly. "This powder may be poison!"

18

Phoney Chemist

SEÑOR VELEZ took Nancy's advice. He laid the wooden handle with the suspicious powder back on the workbench. Nancy walked over and now unscrewed the handle of the fork. It, too, contained the powder.

"I wonder how much of this stuff Luis Llosa shipped," she said. "As soon as the police return, I think we should ask them to get in touch with the New York police and the customs officials there."

"You mean," said George, "that they should investigate Wallace's importing activities?" Nancy nodded.

Just then one of the police officers returned. He said they had not caught Luis Llosa.

"Perhaps he is at this address," said Nancy, and showed the policeman the letters.

"The address on the envelopes is not the one he gave me when he came to work here," observed Señor Velez. "He must have moved."

"Probably Llosa doesn't stay anywhere very long," Nancy commented. "He doesn't want the police to catch up with him."

"We will get him, though, señorita," said one of the officers. He took the letters from Nancy.

The other policeman screwed the handles back on to

the spoon and fork, then put them in a pocket of his jacket.

"I will have these tested and report to Señor Velez and you what is inside."

Soon after the officers had left, the girls took a taxi to the Ponte home. Carla's parents were astounded at the story of what had happened at the shop and in the mountains.

"I am very much worried about you girls," Señora Ponte said. "Perhaps a secret trip—"

Instantly Nancy told of her desire to visit the Nascan lines.

Carla's father said he thought this was a very good idea. "It would be far safer for you girls to 'disappear' for a while than to stay here. I will arrange a camping trip to the desert."

"That would be marvellous," said Nancy.

Señor Ponte said that his company owned a large helicopter. He was sure he could make arrangements to borrow it for the trip.

"It is better to go that way than in a plane because a helicopter can be set down wherever you wish in the desert."

The girls were thrilled by the prospect of visiting the extraordinary place. Nancy was confident that they were getting closer to the solution of the age-old mystery of the plaque.

Señora Ponte told her visitors that several letters had come for them from the United States.

Nancy had received three—one from her father, another from Hannah, and one from Ned Nickerson. In it the young man asked how she was getting along with her bobtailed monkey.

Nancy laughed at the quip, then suddenly snapped her fingers. "Of course. Why didn't I think of that before? The spiralling lines on the other side of the plaque were meant to be the monkey's tail!"

She immediately began to study the spiral lines again. It dawned on her that the tip of the tail was at the centre of the plaque and right in the middle of the crossword cipher.

"I'm sure that means it's the most important part of the mystery," she decided. "That's where we should make our dig. But first we must find the right monkey."

Conversation during a late dinner was confined entirely to the coming trip. Señor Ponte said he had been able to make arrangements with the government and his own company for a real safari.

"Señora Ponte and I are going along with you girls. We have never seen the Nascan lines and I think it is high time that we do so. Our pilot will be Ernesto Monge and his co-pilot, Canejo."

Carla's mother smiled. "I offered to take my cook and the food," she said. "but the company has arranged everything. There will be a steward, named Rico, who will act as camp cook also."

"Oh, this sounds so exciting!" Bess remarked.

George could not resist teasing her cousin. "You mean the trip, or the young men?"

Bess wrinkled her nose at George and disdained to answer. The others laughed.

Then Señor Ponte said, "It will be hot in the desert so we will take poles and awning tops. There will be several sets so we can sleep under some of them and move others around to places where we might want to dig for treasure."

Nancy told of her theory about the tip of the monkey's tail being the most likely spot. All agreed that it was an excellent deduction.

"We'll take along plenty of digging tools, so everyone can make a search," Señor Ponte said.

A short time after dinner was over, the police telephoned a report on the case. Señor Ponte spoke to them and after a long conversation came to tell the others what had transpired.

"The powder in the handles of the wooden fork and spoon was quinine. Quantities of this drug were smuggled into the United States for a most peculiar reason. It seems there is a dishonest chemist up there who owns a small laboratory and factory. He was producing a certain wonder-drug pill for a pharmaceutical company and being handsomely paid.

"The medicine, however, proved to be very expensive to produce, so this chemist began substituting quinine for one of the costly ingredients. The quinine was smuggled into New York by Harry Wallace and sent to the chemist.

"After Wallace had removed the powder from the forks and spoons, he sold the rare arrayánes pieces at a high price. The rest of the shipment, made at the Velez craft shop by Llosa, was fashioned from the common queñar wood and sold through regular channels at a fair figure."

"What a neat racket!" George exclaimed.

Nancy asked, "Did Luis Llosa get the quinine here?"

"Probably," Carla's father replied. "The Lima police believe that Luis Llosa stole his supply of it from various sources in South America."

"I don't see why he went to the trouble of getting

arrayánes wood," George remarked. "He could have used something easy to buy."

"We'll have to find out about that later," Nancy replied. "Señor Ponte, were the other articles in the shipments stolen from Velez's shop?"

"I'm afraid so," her host answered.

"How did the police learn about the wonder-drug racket?" George asked.

Señor Ponte smiled. "Thanks to Nancy Drew," he said. "They contacted United States authorities who picked up Harry Wallace, out on bail. He was at the return address given on the envelopes she found. After a surprise inspection of the chemist's place, he also was arrested."

"Did they find Luis Llosa?" Bess asked.

"No," Señor Ponte replied. "The police learned that he was only boarding at the Lima address on the envelopes. He had not been there for a week."

Bess burst out, "Now that his pals have been caught, maybe he'll get scared and run away. Then he won't bother us any more."

George scoffed. "Don't be silly. He'll be madder than ever and keep after us."

Nancy was inclined to agree with George and wondered what Luis Llosa would do next. She hoped it would be nothing to delay or ruin their trip to the Nascan lines.

"There will be one other passenger I did not tell you about," Señor Ponte said. "He is a government official who is an archaeologist. His name is Dr Benevides."

Soon the group said good night to one another. They were to be up early to make the trip.

The next morning Señor Ponte drove them all to the airfield and there the girls met the men who would be their travelling companions. They were handsome with charming manners, and all spoke English. Nancy and George noted how Bess's eyes sparkled and they winked at each other.

Nancy thought affectionately, "For Bess the expedition is a success even before it starts!"

The helicopter rose gracefully and set off for the pebbly desert in southern Peru. Two hours later the pilot, Ernesto, announced over his microphone that they were nearing the Nascan lines. Immediately the Pontes and their friends crowded to the various windows and gazed below. The co-pilot, Canejo, came back to join them.

"Oh my goodness!" Bess cried out. "Look at that giant!"

She pointed at the outline of a man etched in the ground below. Canejo told her it was eight hundred feet tall.

"There's a fish!" George exclaimed. "A highway is running right through the middle of it!"

Canejo explained that this was the Pan-American Highway which had been built before present-day people realized that among the markings on the desert there were giant figures.

"I see a monkey stretched out on his back," Carla called out. The co-pilot said that this particular figure was two hundred and sixty-two feet in height.

"It is a marvellous bit of work," said Señora Ponte. "This is not like the monkey on our plaque, though."

The whole group was fascinated by the long lines

that looked like roadways. Many of them interlocked. There were also several spirals and huge figures of birds.

"This is the most amazing thing in archaeology I have ever been privileged to see," Señor Ponte remarked.

Dr Benevides agreed wholeheartedly. "The entire project is such a mystery. Everyone wonders why those ancient Indians made their figures so gigantic."

Nancy smiled. "May I venture a guess?" she asked.

"Please do," the doctor said, smiling.

Nancy told him about their trip to Machu Picchu and the elderly Indian who had remarkable eyesight. "He can see objects two-thirds of a mile away. If the ancient Indians who lived around here had that kind of vision, they could easily see the giant figures from far away, and enjoyed doing their artwork on a grand scale."

The archaeologist looked at Nancy with interest. "That is a very sensible theory," he said, "and one I have not heard anybody express. I understand some scientists think that this whole area was a great agricultural calendar for the use of farmers. Or possibly it had something to do with the Nascan religion of the time."

Before Dr Benevides had a chance to make any further comment, Bess gave a shriek of delight.

"Look!" she cried out. "There's our monkey with the spiral tail!"

19

Desert Mummy

EVERYONE in the helicopter gazed down at the monkey figure. It looked exactly like the one on the plaque and the spiralling tail matched perfectly.

Nancy was thrilled. "Oh, I'm sure that figure was carved long ago by the Pontes' ancestor Aguilar!" she thought.

When Nancy told the others her idea, everyone agreed, and Carla said, "I want to see it again!"

The pilot circled the area several times, then asked Señor Ponte if he wished to land.

Before he had a chance to answer, George cried out, "There's a giant cat figure! Cats remind me of Luis Llosa."

Ernesto looked back for a moment. "Did you say Luis Llosa?" he asked.

"Yes."

The pilot said that when he was attending a Peruvian flying school several years before, one of the students there was named Luis Llosa. "He had a cat tattoo on his upper arm."

His listeners were extremely interested. "Please tell us more," said Nancy.

"Luis was a very good parachutist, but as a man he was a troublemaker," the pilot replied. "Finally he was expelled. I have never heard what became of him. Do you know this person?"

"Yes, we do," Nancy answered, and told Ernesto the story. "If you ever see or hear of him, please get in touch with the police immediately."

Ernesto promised to do so, then at a signal from Señor Ponte he landed his helicopter close to the spiral-tailed monkey. The steps were lowered and everyone got out.

"Oh, it's hot!" Bess exclaimed.

Dr Benevides told her that the temperature in this desert varied little. She would soon become adjusted to its warmth.

"Sometimes in the early morning there's a slight mist here, but never any rain or wind."

The archaeologist's prediction that the group would soon adjust to the warm air proved to be true. The poles were set up and the canvas canopies put in place. Then the digging tools were unpacked. The girls expressed their eagerness to start work, but Señor Ponte suggested that they eat lunch first and stay under the shelter of the canvases while the sun was high.

"You will have plenty of time to search," he said. "The sun goes to bed late here."

During the rest period Dr Benevides, the Pontes and their friends discussed where to start the dig. The desert figures had been etched into the ground by removing the top layer of pebbles and piling them along the edges of the wide paths. The two sides of one of the monkey's arms were as far apart as a narrow street!

Although Nancy felt that the tip of the tail was the place where a treasure might be found, Dr Benevides

asked them to start digging in the area where the tail
started to spiral.

"I believe that since the monkey is on one side of the
plaque and most of the tail on the other, this fact has
real significance. Perhaps Aguilar intended to indicate
that the clue to the mystery is at the joining of the
two."

Because of the distance between the two paths
outlining the tail, he had the searchers start digging in
separate places. Work began with a will. Except for the
noise of the tools as they hit the stony ground, there was
not a sound.

The upper layer of pebbles was about two inches
deep and below this lay a stratum of brownish-white
stone. Because of the terrain it was evident that if
Aguilar had hidden something here, it would not be
buried very deep. After going down a couple of feet,
each digger would move to a new position. Hour after
hour went by with no results.

"This is discouraging," Bess complained.

At six o'clock Señor Ponte decided that they should
cease digging for the day. Just then his daughter cried
out excitedly:

"Come, everybody! I have found a mummy!"

"A mummy!" her mother exclaimed.

Everyone hurried to Carla's side. She had uncovered
only the head, which was rather well preserved.
Quickly the men helped to unearth the rest of the
clothed body from its shallow grave. Because of the
dry even climate it had not disintegrated.

Meanwhile, Dr Benevides studied the face. "This
is not the mummy of an ancient Indian," he said. "He
belongs to the white race."

The clothing of the man in the shallow grave proved to be that of a Spanish explorer.

"Whoever buried him did a careful job," the archaeologist remarked.

During the past few seconds Nancy had been thinking hard. Finally she said, "Do you suppose this could possibly be the mummy of your ancestor Aguilar, Señor Ponte?"

The others were startled by the suggestion, but agreed it was quite possible. Aguilar's Indian companion who had delivered the plaque to the Ponte family could have made the burial.

"Perhaps we can find some identification," Dr Benevides suggested. He kneeled on the ground and very carefully unbuttoned the jacket. He turned back one side. A paper stuck out of an inside pocket. "I'm almost afraid to touch this," he said. "It may crumble."

"We must take that chance," said Señor Ponte.

Dr Benevides was used to working meticulously on digs, and the girls marvelled at the deft way he lifted the paper out with forceps. To the onlookers' amazement, the writing on it—in Spanish—was still legible.

Carla's father read it, then said quietly, "This is an honourable discharge from the Spanish army to—" he paused, then finished with a catch in his voice, "to Renato Aguilar."

Everyone looked at the mummy with reverence. No one spoke until Señor Ponte said, "We will re-inter the body. Perhaps it can be removed from here later."

When the brief ceremony was over, the group picked

up their tools and walked back to the tents. Soon Rico had supper ready.

"And I am hungry," declared Señor Ponte. "The desert air has given me an appetite."

Later, when the girls were preparing for bed, Nancy remarked, "I am more convinced than ever that Aguilar came here to bury his treasure. He did not dare entrust it to his Indian servant because he might have been attacked by bandits and the object— whatever it is—stolen from him."

George nodded in agreement. "I doubt that Aguilar thought it would take so long for his family to figure out the crossword cipher."

Nancy smiled. "We haven't figured it out yet."

"But in the morning," said Bess, "we will!"

The campers were awake early and as soon as breakfast was over the searchers walked to new digging positions. Before they had a chance to reach the spots, they became aware of an approaching plane. It was fairly large and flying slowly.

As they watched, a parachutist jumped from it. In a few moments his chute billowed out and he drifted down to land near the camp.

"What does he want?" George asked.

Within seconds, another parachutist dropped from the plane; then, one by one, several more. When all had hit the ground they quickly unharnessed themselves and hurried towards the campers.

The leader was a thin, heavily bearded man with bushy black hair. In a deep voice he said, "I am sorry to disturb you, but in the name of the Peruvian government you are under arrest. Get into the helicopter and my men will take you back to Lima.

Nancy and her companions were stunned. Immediately Dr Benevides said, "But we have permission from the government to dig here."

"The permission has been cancelled," the bearded parachutist said. "Now do not make any trouble. Leave everything here and get in the helicopter."

Nancy had been watching the beady eyes of the leader and strongly suspected that he might be Luis Llosa in disguise. She edged towards the pilot and his co-pilot, and whispered her suspicions to them. Instantly they lunged forward and seized the intruder.

"Now," said Ernesto, "we'll see if you have a cat tattoo on your arm."

"And maybe that hair and beard will come off," added Canejo, reaching towards the whiskers.

"Leave that man alone!" barked one of the suspect's companions as they closed in belligerently.

At the same time, their leader jerked free and swung a blow at Ernesto. Instantly the other parachutists leaped on the pilots and Rico.

Señor Ponte was yelling at the top of his voice for everyone to calm down. "We want no trouble!" he cried out.

Another parachutist, a very tall, heavy-set man, picked Nancy up in his arms and raced towards the helicopter. There he whirled and called out:

"You will do what I say or I will take this girl away as a hostage!"

· 20 ·

An Imposter's Story

"OH, Nancy! No! No!" Bess shrieked. "Don't let them take you away!"

"They won't!" Ernesto cried.

The parachutists had not counted on the strength of the men in Nancy's group, nor George's knowledge of judo. Ernesto dashed to Nancy's rescue. With a stinging blow, the pilot knocked out the big fellow who was holding her.

By this time Luis Llosa's disguise had been yanked off and he stood clean-shaven and short-haired. One of his khaki shirt sleeves was ripped, revealing a cat tattoo on his arm! He stood alone for a moment, panting, while Canejo went to help subdue the intruders. Suddenly Llosa started to run.

Bess whispered to her cousin, "Get him!"

George did not hesitate. To Llosa's utter surprise, she rushed up and used one of her judo holds on him. He went head over heels—and even Señora Ponte, startled as she was, had to smile.

As Nancy came running back to the other girls, Ernesto joined the fight again. It was about even, with neither side winning.

Then, suddenly, Luis Llosa got up from the

ground and called out, "I give up! Cut the fighting!"

The mêlée stopped and the smuggler faced the Pontes and their friends.

"I want all of you to stand back and listen. We mean no harm. All we want is to get out of here. My friends and I will take the helicopter and send someone back for you."

"The nerve of him!" George burst out.

"He's afraid we'll overpower him," Nancy thought, "and turn him over to the police."

Quickly she stepped forward and addressed Luis Llosa's companions. "Do you know that this man is a smuggler wanted by the police? That he's a thief?"

"It is true," Carla spoke up. "And he tried several times to injure my friend." She put her hand on Nancy's arm.

Luis Llosa's eyes blazed. "Do not believe what she says!" he shouted to the other parachutists.

But by now his so-called friends were backing away from him. One of them declared he knew nothing about any of this.

"Llosa told us if we would come along, he would show us where a great treasure was buried in this desert. He said he was a government official."

"He is nothing of the sort!" George retorted. "He's El Gato!"

Llosa gazed from one to another of his grimly silent companions, then looked back at the other group.

"I see I am cornered," he said bitterly, realizing that there was no one to help him. "I will tell my story and then leave."

Nancy suppressed a smile. "That's what you think," she murmured to herself.

She had noticed Ernesto going to the helicopter. When he had climbed inside, she was sure he was going to radio the federal police to come and pick up the intruders.

"I admit," said Llosa, "to being El Gato, head of a smuggling ring," He turned to Nancy with a sneer on his face. "Thanks to you, several of my men are in jail."

She made no comment except to ask if Señor Jorge Velez was entirely innocent. Luis Llosa assured her he was.

Carla asked, "Why did you use the arrayánes wood and where did you get it?"

Llosa said that the small pieces of it had been taken regularly—but unobtrusively—from the forest by Wagner and shipped to him.

"Since it looked very different from the other wood used for the salad forks and spoons, Wallace could identify it easily in New York when he opened the shipments. Besides, it was a clever way to send the quinine."

Llosa revealed that Wallace had asked a friend who had visited him at the jail to phone the message about the girls' cancelled flight. And it was Sanchez who who had thrown the rock that hit Nancy.

"What about the plaque?" she asked. "How did you become interested in that?"

The captured man said he had overheard Señor Ponte and Señora Ponte talking about the plaque in a restaurant. They had said it might lead to something valuable if deciphered. The couple were a little concerned that they had let their daughter Carla take it with her, but she had wanted the plaque to remind her of home.

"When I learned that the girl had gone to River Heights, I wrote my friend Harry Wallace to get it. Everything seemed to be going all right after he scared her by sending 'the cat' note. And he followed her a few times and eavesdropped.

"That is how he knew she took the plaque to Miss Drew's house. When Wallace heard she was a girl detective, he had to think up some way to get the plaque so she could not find out its secret."

Llosa admitted that Sanchez had been able to make a sketch of it at the Hotel Llao-Llao. "But he had some bad luck there. That stupid shop owner hung it on a wall and of course Miss Drew discovered it."

"Who was the man who tried to kidnap Carla," Nancy asked, "and why did he do it?"

"He was Wagner's friend, Ramon Ruiz," Llosa answered. "Sanchez sent him to pick a few pockets at the casino, but when the girl started asking questions about Sanchez, he thought it would be a good idea to take her along and find out what she was up to.

"He was the one who tampered with the plane door," Luis added, and explained that Ruiz was a petty crook who worked as a part-time mechanic at the Bariloche airport. "Before Sanchez was arrested, he gave Ruiz orders to loosen the door's hinges. The police can pick Ruiz up any night at the casino.

"I had even worse luck," the smuggler went on in a whining tone. "I hired an Indian boy from a mountain village to follow Miss Drew in Cuzco, but he was frightened off by the earthquake. A man at Machu Picchu failed me too."

Luis stopped speaking and there was silence for a few moments. Then the prisoner glared at Nancy and said, "To be outwitted by a girl—!"

Bess tossed her head. "It's too bad you didn't find out at the start how clever Nancy is. You would have saved yourself a lot of trouble."

A second later the whirring of a helicopter's rotors could be heard, and in a few minutes the craft landed. Several federal police officers stepped out and Llosa and his companions were hustled aboard. His "friends" were still declaring their innocence, but the police said this would have to be proved.

After the helicopter was a mere speck in the sky, Nancy and her friends once more turned to thoughts of unearthing a treasure. Dr Benevides, concluding that his theory of where to look had been wrong, smilingly said that this time Nancy was to have her way. They would dig in the area at the tip of the monkey's tail. The men started the work, but when they had gone about as deep as they thought something might be buried, Señor Ponte handed Nancy a trowel.

"If there is anything here, you should have the honour of uncovering it, my dear," he said.

Nancy tried not to appear over-eager, but her heart was pounding with excitement. Dropping to her knees, she began to take out the hard dirt little by little.

In moments Nancy was sure that she had hit something other than stone. She began working a little faster but still very carefully.

Finally Nancy said, "There *is* something here."

The others crowded around as she picked up an archaeologist's dusting brush and swept it over a four-inch-square section.

"Gold!" Bess cried.

Everyone offered to help Nancy, who now was smiling broadly. "I think the Pontes should have the honour of uncovering whatever was buried here by their ancestor Aguilar," she said.

Carla and her father picked up tools. Señora Ponte watched.

Finally a solid-gold box about eighteen inches long, eight inches wide and twelve inches high was unearthed. The lid was sealed tight and it took the searchers some time, using a very fine chisel and hammer, to get the top loose.

"Nancy, this is really your find," said Señor Ponte. "You open it."

The young detective demurred. "It belongs to you," she said.

Carla settled the matter. "Suppose the three of us raise the lid together."

The others watched tensely as this was done.

"It *is* a treasure!" Señor Ponte exclaimed.

There were murmers of excitement and awe when the onlookers saw the contents.

Bess blinked hard. "I am so happy I could cry!"

Inside the box were several solid gold objects of Inca design. The largest one was of a monkey with a spiralling tail.

"This is a priceless collection!" Dr Benevides exclaimed excitedly.

One by one the objects were lifted out and examined.

Nancy had noticed folded papers in the bottom of the box.

"May I take these out?" she asked Señor Ponte.

"Indeed you may."

There were two "papers". Carefully Nancy unfolded the first one. It was a large drawing. She held it up for everyone to see.

"Buildings," Bess remarked. "Where are they?"

Nancy was staring intently at the drawing. In a lower corner she detected faded writing.

After carefully scrutinizing it, she exclaimed excitedly, "This is a drawing of Machu Picchu—the way it must have looked before it was sacked!"

"How magnificent it looks on top of the mountain!" Señor Ponte burst out.

"And look!" George cried. "Here is a portrait of the Inca ruler at the time, son of the sun god!"

Dr Benevides was beside himself with delight. "This is the most amazing and valuable find of the century!" he said.

Everyone began to talk at once. Did these priceless objects and drawings belong to the Pontes or to the Peruvian government?

Carla's father said firmly, "No matter whom they belong to, I think they should be shared with the world. These drawings, in particular, should be kept in a fireproof museum."

"I can assure you," said Dr Benevides, "that is exactly what the government will want."

"Poor Aguilar!" said Bess. "He must have known he was dying and would never get home again. That would explain why he carved the plaque for his family."

"I think you're right," Nancy replied. She gazed out over the desert, trying to imagine the long ago events. "Maybe after he and the Indian had buried the treasure, they made camp here. Aguilar's strength was gone, but he managed to carve the plaque before he died."

Señor Ponte agreed. "And he put the message in code so that if robbers attacked the Indian, they could not learn about the treasure."

"Probably," Carla added. "Since the Indian did not speak Spanish, he could not explain anything to the family. He could only leave the plaque with them."

"How pleased Aguilar would be," Señora Ponte said softly, "to know that his message has been deciphered at last!"

When the excitement died down, Nancy began to feel rather pensive—a feeling she always had when a mystery was completely solved. She hoped that another challenging case would come along soon. And it did when Nancy and her friends became involved in *The Quest of the Missing Map*.

"One thing we are forgetting," Carla spoke up, "is that if it had not been for Nancy Drew, this treasure probably never would have come to light." She turned to her new friend and hugged her. "You are the most wonderful girl in the world. Nancy, you have actually solved a three-hundred-year-old mystery!"

As Nancy blushed at the praise, the men shook her hand, but Señora Ponte and the girls embraced her.

"I didn't do it alone," she said. "A lot of credit goes to my very special friends."

Bess smiled, then began to examine the drawing of Machu Picchu. A minute later she put one finger on a certain spot. "Nancy," she said, "this is where you almost lost your life."

George looked disapprovingly at her cousin. "For Pete's sake, Bess, why can't you think of something cheerful?"

"Like what?"

"Like—like every time I see a monkey with a spiralling tail, I'll think of Nancy and her mystery in Peru!"

CAPTAIN ARMADA

has a whole shipload of exciting books for you

Armadas are chosen by children all over the world. They're designed to fit your pocket, and your pocket money too – and they make terrific presents for friends. They're colourful, exciting, and there are hundreds of titles to choose from – thrilling mysteries, spooky ghost stories, hilarious joke books, brain-teasing quizzes and puzzles, fascinating hobby books, stories about ponies and schools – and many, many more. Armada has something for everyone.

Book Tokens

Give them the pleasure of choosing

Book Tokens can be bought and exchanged at most bookshops.

Armada